ETS. TOEIC.

TOEIC®
Listening and Reading Test
Official Test-Preparation Guide Vol. **8**

Listening Part

TOEIC® 聽力與閱讀測驗[1]於 1979 年首次推出,為英語教育測驗界帶來許多重大且正面的影響。40 多年來,TOEIC 系列測驗為評估工作場所和日常生活所需的英語溝通技能設立了標準。全球有超過 160 個國家、14,000 家企業或機構,認同 TOEIC 測驗能夠準確評估應試者是否具備在日常生活或工作中,有效地使用英語與他人交流的能力和技能。

作為全球最大的教育測驗機構之一,ETS® 非常重視試題研發的品質。TOEIC 測驗的每一道題目,都有至少一個被設定好的目標能力(Abilities Measured),聽力測驗和閱讀測驗分別測量五種不同的能力。從 TOEIC 聽力與閱讀測驗成績單中的 Abilities Measured 部分[2],應試者可以看到自己在每項目標能力的答對比例,進而針對該項英語目標能力做專長發揮或是能力補強。

長期以來,台灣的教學環境習慣以一個量化的結果(分數)作為學習的終點,而較少關注產生結果的過程,或是結果所代表的意義。這就是第八冊《TOEIC® 聽力與閱讀測驗官方全真試題指南》的起源。有別於過去僅提供解析的官方指南,第八冊清楚地說明了每一道題目的目標能力,希望讓準備要參加 TOEIC 測驗的應試者,藉由了解目標能力,發揮並改善自己的強項與弱項,提升溝通實力,強化個人競爭力,循序漸進地達到期望的結果;而教學者也可以透過目標能力,設定合適的教學目標與教學內容,讓教學與學習的結果都更具有實質意義。

第八冊同樣提供兩套全真模擬試題,並將聽力與閱讀分開出版,在聚焦學習的同時獲得最佳成效。期盼教學者、學習者、應試者都能利用本書,在英語學習的路上持續邁進,運用在生活及工作當中,成為能使用英語溝通的國際人才。

TOEIC® 臺灣區總代理　忠欣股份有限公司 董事長

 謹識

---

[1] TOEIC 全名為 Test of English for International Communication,
　TOEIC 系列測驗分為聽力與閱讀測驗及口說與寫作測驗。其中口說及寫作測驗可分開選擇。

[2] 可參閱本書 P.9 目標能力(Abilities Measured)說明。

　　本書收錄兩套 *TOEIC*® 聽力與閱讀測驗的聽力全真試題，每套各有 100 道題目，和實際測驗相同。在練習全真試題之後，可根據第 54、55 頁提供的分數換算表、目標能力正答率計算方式及目標能力對應，獲得參考的結果。最後則提供題目中文翻譯、重點解析及各項目標能力說明。

題型範例

　　提供聽力測驗試題範例以及應答說明，讓讀者理解 TOEIC 聽力測驗各題型的測驗方式。

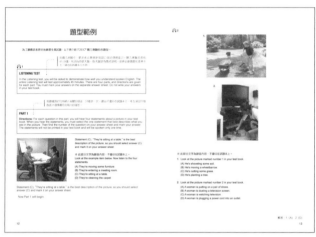

▲ 聽力測驗

全真試題

　　共有兩套全真試題，內容與實際測驗相同，聽力測驗有 100 題，可使用書中所附的模擬答案卡作答，並試著在 45 分鐘之限制時間內，完成所有題目。

▲ 全真試題

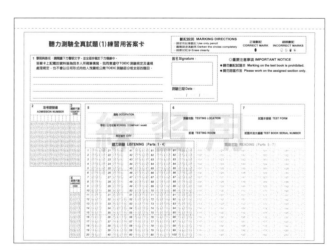

▲ 答案卡

分數及目標能力計算

　　測驗完畢後可依照第 51 頁開始的「試題解答與分數及目標能力計算」，計算出分數及目標能力正答率。需注意的是，本書所提供的分數換算方式僅適用於 *ETS®* 所提供的全真模擬試題，與實際測驗的成績計算方法不同，故本書獲得的分數為參考分數。

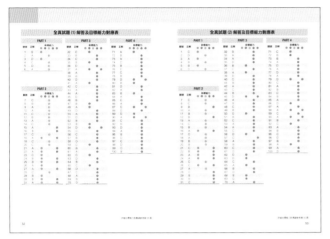

▲ 試題解答

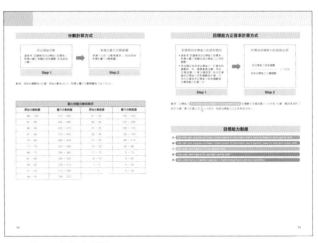

▲ 分數及目標能力計算

中文翻譯及目標能力解析

　　提供每一道題目的中文翻譯、詳盡解析，並標示出各題所要評量的目標能力及應試重點。

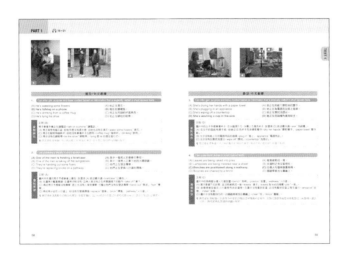

測驗簡介

　　TOEIC 聽力與閱讀測驗是 TOEIC Program 的一員，專為英語非母語人士測試英語聽力與閱讀能力。測驗內容主要是檢測職場情境或日常生活中所需的英語能力，考生不需具備特定專業知識或字彙。本項測驗的試題都經過一系列審查，排除不了解特定文化就無法理解的內容，以確保試題的公平性，適合全世界的考生受測。

測驗題型

　　測驗內容分成聽力（約 45 分鐘，100 題）和閱讀（75 分鐘，100 題）兩部分，各題型及題數如下表所示。

聽力測驗（Listening Section）測驗時間：約 45 分鐘		
大題	內容	題數
1	照片描述　Photographs	6
2	應答問題　Question-Response	25
3	簡短對話　Conversations	39（共 13 個題組，每題組有 3 題）
4	簡短獨白　Talks	30（共 10 個題組，每題組有 3 題）
	總計	100

閱讀測驗（Reading Section）測驗時間：75 分鐘		
大題	內容	題數
5	句子填空　Incomplete Sentences	30
6	段落填空　Text Completion	16
7	單篇閱讀　Single Passages	29（共 10 個題組，每題組有 2～4 題）
	多篇閱讀　Multiple Passages	25（共 5 個題組，每題組有 5 題）
	總計	100

成績單說明

　　成績單主要由三個項目所組成，包括（1）考生基本資訊及成績、（2）聽力測驗及閱讀測驗的能力論述說明、（3）目標能力的正答率。考生可藉由能力論述及目標能力正答率，了解所得分數代表的對應能力，以及自身英語能力的強弱項。

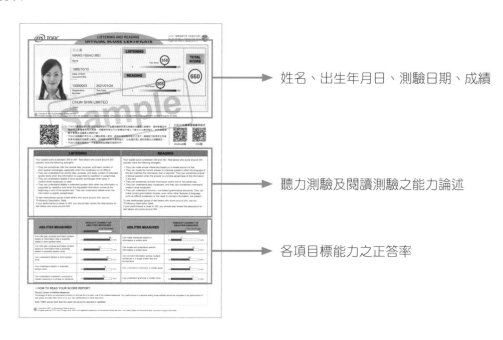

姓名、出生年月日、測驗日期、成績

聽力測驗及閱讀測驗之能力論述

各項目標能力之正答率

分數計算

　　TOEIC 聽力與閱讀測驗分數是使用實驗驗證的統計等化程序（equating），將答對題數所得的原始分數（raw score）轉換成量尺分數（scaled score），答錯不倒扣。測驗本身沒有所謂的「通過」或「不通過」，而是將受測者的能力以聽力 5 ～ 495 分、閱讀 5 ～ 495 分、總分 10 ～ 990 分的分數來呈現。藉由換算程序，即使是不同次的測驗，所得出的分數意義是相同的。也就是說，某次測驗得分 550 分，和另外一次測驗得分 550 分，代表著相同的英語能力。

目標能力（Abilities Measured）

　　TOEIC 聽力與閱讀測驗在聽力及閱讀部份各有 5 項不同的目標能力：

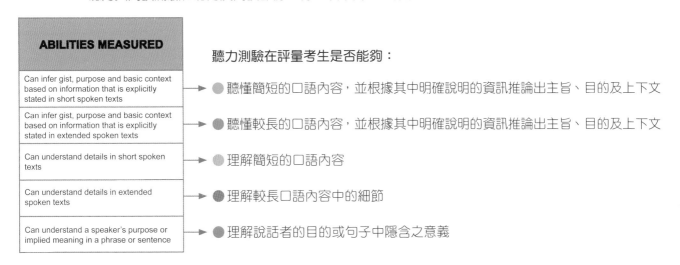

ABILITIES MEASURED

Can infer gist, purpose and basic context based on information that is explicitly stated in short spoken texts
Can infer gist, purpose and basic context based on information that is explicitly stated in extended spoken texts
Can understand details in short spoken texts
Can understand details in extended spoken texts
Can understand a speaker's purpose or implied meaning in a phrase or sentence

聽力測驗在評量考生是否能夠：

● 聽懂簡短的口語內容，並根據其中明確說明的資訊推論出主旨、目的及上下文

● 聽懂較長的口語內容，並根據其中明確說明的資訊推論出主旨、目的及上下文

● 理解簡短的口語內容

● 理解較長口語內容中的細節

● 理解說話者的目的或句子中隱含之意義

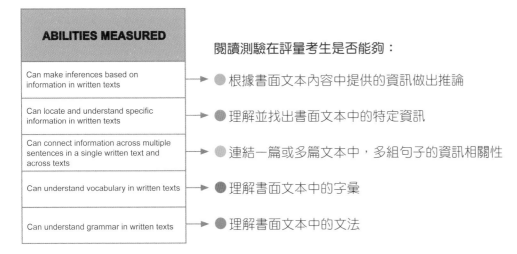

ABILITIES MEASURED

Can make inferences based on information in written texts
Can locate and understand specific information in written texts
Can connect information across multiple sentences in a single written text and across texts
Can understand vocabulary in written texts
Can understand grammar in written texts

閱讀測驗在評量考生是否能夠：

● 根據書面文本內容中提供的資訊做出推論

● 理解並找出書面文本中的特定資訊

● 連結一篇或多篇文本中，多組句子的資訊相關性

● 理解書面文本中的字彙

● 理解書面文本中的文法

目標能力正答率

　　目標能力正答率是 TOEIC 聽力與閱讀測驗成績單中的一個項目，是由應試者在各項目標能力對應試題中的答對數量計算而來，在成績單上使用長條圖來呈現。假設某題本中，使用 20 道題目來評量考生某項目標能力，而考生答對了其中 11 題，則該目標能力之正答率為 55%。正答率之比例只能與參加同一次 TOEIC 聽力與閱讀測驗的考生進行比較，由於某些能力的問題數量相對較少，因此在比較時應謹慎。

能力論述

TOEIC 聽力測驗成績對應能力論述

分數	強項	弱項
400	**簡短口語內容：** • 能從廣泛的詞彙中，推論出主旨、目的及基本的上下文。在對話內容不直接或難以預測時，也不影響其理解。 • 能夠理解內容細節，使用複雜的句子結構及困難字彙時，也不影響其理解。 **較長口語內容：** • 能夠推論出主旨、目的及上下文。即使不重複或不多加解釋時，也能理解其對話內容。 • 能夠連結不同資訊間的關聯性，並由解釋的方式理解其內容細節，在對話內容不重複或包含否定語句時，也不影響其理解。	• 僅在使用不常見或困難的文法及字彙時，才會出現問題。
300	**簡短口語內容：** • 能從廣泛的詞彙中，推論出主旨、目的及基本的上下文，特別是字彙程度不難的時候。 • 能夠理解並且使用簡單或中等程度字彙的口語內容細節。 **較長口語內容：** • 透過說話者重複或解釋，能夠推論出較長內容的主旨、目的以及基本的上下文。 • 當重點資訊出現在句首或句尾，並被重複說明的時候，能理解其內容細節。若訊息被稍加解釋，也能理解其細節。	**簡短口語內容：** • 若對話內容不直接、難以預測或使用困難字彙時，難以理解其主旨、目的或基本的上下文。 • 無法理解包含複雜的語法結構或者困難字彙的口語交流，亦無法理解包含否定結構的細節。 **較長口語內容：** • 當需要連結不同訊息，或使用困難字彙的時候，無法理解其主旨、目的或基本的上下文。 • 當訊息不重複或需要連結不同訊息時，無法理解其內容的細節。無法理解大多數需要透過解釋的內容或較困難的文法架構。
200	**簡短口語內容：** • 在簡短（一句話）描述的狀況下，能夠理解照片的主旨。 • 使用的字彙較簡單且只有少量必須理解的內容時，能理解簡短口語交流和照片描述中的細節。 **較長口語內容：** • 如果訊息被大量重複並使用簡單的字彙，有時候能推論出較長內容的主旨、目的及基本的上下文。 • 當被要求的資訊出現在句首或是句尾並與問題所使用的語言相同時，能夠理解其內容細節。	**簡短口語內容：** • 即使內容直接且沒有難以預測的訊息，仍無法理解其主旨、目的或基本的上下文。 • 當使用較困難的單字或複雜的文法結構時，無法理解其內容細節。無法理解包含否定結構的細節。 **較長口語內容：** • 當需要連結不同訊息，或使用困難字彙的時候，無法理解其主旨、目的或基本的上下文。 • 當被要求的訊息出現在文本中時，無法理解其細節，亦無法理解經過解釋的訊息或者困難的文法結構。

TOEIC 閱讀測驗成績對應能力論述

分數	強項	弱項
450	• 能夠推斷書面文本的主旨及目的，也能夠對細節做出推論。 • 能夠透過閱讀理解書面文本的含意，即使內容被經過解釋，也能理解真實訊息。 • 能夠連結同篇或是多篇文章中的不同訊息。 • 能夠理解廣泛的字彙，常用字少見的用法及片語的使用，也可以分辨相似詞之間的差異。 • 能夠理解有規則的文法架構，也可以理解困難、複雜或少見的句子結構。	• 在測驗的訊息特別密集或者牽涉到特別困難的字彙時，才會出現問題。
350	• 能夠推論書面文本的主旨及目的，也能夠對細節做出推論。 • 能夠透過閱讀理解書面文本的含意，即使內容被經過解釋，也能理解真實訊息。 • 即使使用較難的字彙或是文法，也能夠連結同篇文本中小範圍的資訊。 • 能理解中等程度的字彙，有時能藉由上下文理解困難的字彙、常用字少見的用法和片語的使用。 • 能夠理解有規則的文法結構，也可以理解困難、複雜或少見的句子架構。	• 無法將同篇文章內大範圍的訊息做連結。 • 無法完全理解困難的字彙、常用字少見的用法或是片語的使用。通常無法分辨出相似詞之間的差異。
250	• 能夠在有限的書面文本中做出簡單的推論。 • 當文本使用的語言與所需訊息相符時，可以找到真實訊息的正確答案。當答案是對文本訊息的簡單解釋時，有時可以回答關於事實的問題。 • 有時能連結單一或是兩個句子之間的訊息。 • 能夠理解簡單的字彙，有時候也能理解中等程度的字彙。 • 能夠理解常見或者具有規則的文法結構，即使在使用有難度的字彙或需要連結訊息時，仍能選出正確的文法選項。	• 無法理解需要透過解釋或者連結訊息所做出的推論。 • 使用困難的字彙解釋時，理解實際訊息的能力十分有限，需要依靠在文本中找出與問題相同的字詞來答題。 • 通常無法連結超過兩句的訊息。 • 無法理解困難的字彙、常用字少見的用法或是片語的使用，無法分辨出相似詞之間的差異。 • 無法理解更加困難、複雜或少見的文法架構。
150	• 當所需的閱讀量不多，且文本使用的語言與問題相同時，能夠找到正確的答案。 • 能夠理解簡單的字彙以及基本的慣用語。 • 在所需閱讀量不多時，能夠理解最常見並且具有規則的文法架構。	• 無法根據書面文本的訊息做出推論。 • 無法理解經過解釋的事實與訊息，必須依靠在文本中找出與問題相同的字詞來答題。 • 就算在單一句子裡，仍經常無法連結訊息。 • 能夠理解的字彙十分有限。 • 當使用較難的字彙或者需要連結訊息時，即使文法句構簡單亦無法理解。

題型範例

為了讓應試者更好地練習全真試題，以下將介紹 *TOEIC®* 聽力測驗的各題型。

在聽力測驗中，要求考生展現對英語口說的理解能力。聽力測驗全長約 45 分鐘，共分為四個大題，每大題皆有應考說明。答案必須填寫在答案卡上，請勿在試題本上作答。

🎧 1

LISTENING TEST

In the Listening test, you will be asked to demonstrate how well you understand spoken English. The entire Listening test will last approximately 45 minutes. There are four parts, and directions are given for each part. You must mark your answers on the separate answer sheet. Do not write your answers in your test book.

每題播放四句與照片相關的描述，只播放一次。題目不會印在試題本上，考生須從四個敘述中選擇最符合照片的描述。

PART 1

Directions: For each question in this part, you will hear four statements about a picture in your test book. When you hear the statements, you must select the one statement that best describes what you see in the picture. Then find the number of the question on your answer sheet and mark your answer. The statements will not be printed in your test book and will be spoken only one time.

Statement (C), "They're sitting at a table," is the best description of the picture, so you should select answer (C) and mark it on your answer sheet.

※ 此部分文字為錄音內容，不會印在試題本上。
Look at the example item below. Now listen to the four statements.

(A) They're moving some furniture.
(B) They're entering a meeting room.
(C) They're sitting at a table.
(D) They're cleaning the carpet.

Statement (C), "They're sitting at a table," is the best description of the picture, so you should select answer (C) and mark it on your answer sheet.

Now Part 1 will begin.

2

1.

2.

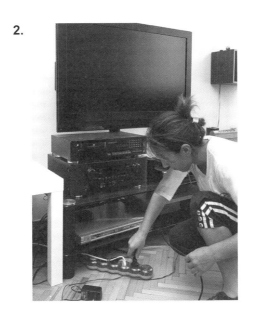

解答：1. (A)　2. (D)

※ 此部分文字為錄音內容，不會印在試題本上。

1. Look at the picture marked number 1 in your test book.

   (A) He's shoveling some soil.
   (B) He's moving a wheelbarrow.
   (C) He's cutting some grass.
   (D) He's planting a tree.

2. Look at the picture marked number 2 in your test book.

   (A) A woman is putting on a pair of shoes.
   (B) A woman is dusting a television screen.
   (C) A woman is watching television.
   (D) A woman is plugging a power cord into an outlet.

PART 2

Directions: You will hear a question or statement and three responses spoken in English. They will not be printed in your test book and will be spoken only one time. Select the best response to the question or statement and mark the letter (A), (B), or (C) on your answer sheet.

🎧 4

7. Mark your answer on your answer sheet.
8. Mark your answer on your answer sheet.
9. Mark your answer on your answer sheet.
10. Mark your answer on your answer sheet.

※ 此部分文字為錄音內容，不會印在試題本上。

7. Where's the new fax machine?

(A) Next to the water fountain.
(B) I'll send a fax tomorrow.
(C) By Wednesday.

8. How well does Thomas play the violin?

(A) Sure, I really like it.
(B) Oh, he's a professional.
(C) I'll turn down the volume.

9. Martin, are you driving to the client meeting?

(A) Oh, would you like a ride?
(B) Nice to meet you, too.
(C) I thought it went well!

10. Mariko announced that she's retiring in April.

(A) How many did you count?
(B) I'm not tired at all.
(C) Right, she's been here twenty-five years.

解答：7. (A)　8. (B)　9. (A)　10. (C)

每題播放一段兩人或兩人以上的對話，每段對話會有三個問題，對話及問題只播放一次，且對話內容不會印在試題本上。考生須在聽完對話並閱讀試題本上的問題及選項後，從四個選項選出最適合的答案。

PART 3

Directions: You will hear some conversations between two or more people. You will be asked to answer three questions about what the speakers say in each conversation. Select the best response to each question and mark the letter (A), (B), (C), or (D) on your answer sheet. The conversations will not be printed in your test book and will be spoken only one time.

 6

32. Why is the woman calling?

    (A) To cancel an order
    (B) To complain about a product
    (C) To redeem a gift card
    (D) To renew a warranty

33. What does the man ask the woman about?

    (A) A model name
    (B) A brand of coffee
    (C) A catalog number
    (D) A date of purchase

34. What does the man offer to do?

    (A) Provide a discount
    (B) Send a free sample
    (C) Extend a warranty
    (D) Issue a refund

※ 此部分文字為錄音內容，不會印在試題本上。

Questions 32 through 34 refer to the following conversation.

W: Hello. I'm calling about a coffee machine I purchased from your Web site. It stopped working even though I haven't had it for very long. I expected it to last much longer than this.

M: Oh, I'm sorry to hear that. Our warranty covers products for up to a year. Do you know when you bought it?

W: I've had it for a little over a year, so the warranty has probably just expired. This is so disappointing.

M: Well, I'll tell you what we can do. Although we can't replace it, since you're a valued customer I can offer you a coupon for forty percent off your next purchase.

解答：32. (B)　33.(D)　34.(A)

35. Where do the speakers work?

    (A) At a hotel
    (B) At a department store
    (C) At a restaurant
    (D) At a call center

36. What does the man ask about?

    (A) How many people have applied for a promotion
    (B) If a manager is in the lobby
    (C) Whether a position is available
    (D) When new shifts will be assigned

37. What does the woman say the man should be prepared to do?

    (A) Handle customer complaints
    (B) Work within a budget
    (C) Get to know local clients
    (D) Work evening hours

※ 此部分文字為錄音內容，不會印在試題本上。

Questions 35 through 37 refer to the following conversation.

M：Oh, hi Yolanda—I'm surprised to see you at the front desk this late. Don't you usually work at the hotel in the morning?

W：Actually, I'm going to be working the evening shift for a while; I'm covering for a front-desk supervisor who was just promoted, but only until the hotel hires a permanent replacement.

M：Oh, so there's a front-desk supervisor position open? I've been looking for a chance to take on a managerial role. Are they still accepting applications?

W：Yes, and if you don't mind working evening hours, I think you have a good chance at the job. I'd contact the manager right now, though—she's starting interviews this week.

解答：35. (A)　36. (C)　37. (D)

38. What is the conversation mainly about?

    (A) An enlargement of office space
    (B) A move into a new market
    (C) An increase in staff numbers
    (D) A change in company leadership

39. Why does the woman say, "I can't believe it"?

    (A) She strongly disagrees.
    (B) She would like an explanation.
    (C) She feels disappointed.
    (D) She is happily surprised.

40. What do the men imply about the company?

    (A) It was recently founded.
    (B) It is planning to adjust salaries.
    (C) It is in a good financial situation.
    (D) It has offices in other countries.

※ 此部分文字為錄音內容，不會印在試題本上。

Questions 38 through 40 refer to the following conversation with three speakers.

M： Have you two taken a look at the progress they've made upstairs on the office expansion? It looks great!

W： I know! I can't believe it! And the offices up there have amazing views of the city.

M： I wonder which division will move up there when it's finished.

W： I heard it's the research department.

M： Ah, because they have the most people.

W： Probably. I'd love to have an office on that floor, though.

M： Yeah. Well, the company must be making good money if they're adding that space!

M： I think you're right, there!

解答：38. (A)　39.(D)　40.(C)

Screen Size	System Price
11 inches	$799
13 inches	$899
15 inches	$999
17 inches	$1,099

41. What does the woman ask the man to do?

    (A) Order some equipment
    (B) Find a new vendor
    (C) Repair a laptop
    (D) Contact a job candidate

42. What problem does the man mention?

    (A) A designer has left the company.
    (B) A supplier has increased its prices.
    (C) A computer model has been discontinued.
    (D) A departmental budget has been reduced.

43. Look at the graphic. What size screen will the man order?

    (A) 11 inches
    (B) 13 inches
    (C) 15 inches
    (D) 17 inches

※ 此部分文字為錄音內容，不會印在試題本上。

Questions 41 through 43 refer to the following conversation and list.

W: Larry, we have a new graphic designer starting next month and we'll need to set her up with a laptop and extra monitor. Can you place orders for those?

M: Sure. You know our vendor has raised their prices, right?

W: Really?

M: Yes. I just looked at the catalog a few minutes ago, and their current models are more expensive.

W: Right. Well, our budget per work area is $1,000 maximum. So let's order the system with the largest screen that falls within that price.

M: OK. I'll take a look at the prices again and place the order.

解答：41. (A)　42. (B)　43. (C)

每題播放一段獨白，每段獨白會有三個問題，獨白及問題只播放一次，且獨白內容不會印在試題本上。考生須在聽完對話並閱讀試題本上的問題及選項後，從四個選項選出最適合的答案。

PART 4

Directions: You will hear some talks given by a single speaker. You will be asked to answer three questions about what the speaker says in each talk. Select the best response to each question and mark the letter (A), (B), (C), or (D) on your answer sheet. The talks will not be printed in your test book and will be spoken only one time.

 11

71. What does the speaker say about the repair?

(A) It is not required.
(B) It has been finished early.
(C) It will be inexpensive.
(D) It is covered by a warranty.

72. When can the listener pick up his car?

(A) Today
(B) Tomorrow
(C) Next week
(D) In two weeks

73. What does the speaker offer to do?

(A) Look for a used part
(B) Refund the cost of a charge
(C) Send an invoice
(D) Arrange a ride

※ 此部分文字為錄音內容，不會印在試題本上。

Questions 71 through 73 refer to the following telephone message.

Hello Mr. Lee, this is Thomas from BKS Auto Shop calling with some information about your car repair. I know we told you that it would take until next week to get the part we ordered, but we got the part early, and I was able to finish the repair. We're going to be closing for the day in a few minutes, but you're welcome to come get your car anytime tomorrow. If you need a ride to the shop tomorrow, let me know, and I can arrange one for you.

解答：71. (B)　72.(B)　73.(D)

74. What kind of business does the speaker work for?

    (A) A restaurant

    (B) A supermarket

    (C) A furniture store

    (D) A fitness center

75. Why does the speaker assign extra work to the listeners?

    (A) A deadline is approaching.

    (B) A staff member is unwell.

    (C) Many customers are expected.

    (D) Equipment needs to be unpacked.

76. What does the speaker ask listeners to tell customers about?

    (A) New business hours

    (B) Discount cards

    (C) A special dish

    (D) A holiday sale

※ 此部分文字為錄音內容，不會印在試題本上。

Questions 74 through 76 refer to the following telephone message.

OK, before you start serving food, I want to let you know that the restaurant is a bit understaffed tonight. Tamara called me this afternoon to let me know that she has a cold. So I'm asking each of you to be in charge of one extra table tonight. Please also remember to tell each table of guests about our new menu special—it's a rice dish with assorted grilled vegetables. I think it'll be very popular because many of our customers have been asking for more vegetarian options. That's all for tonight.

解答：74. (A)　75. (B)　76. (C)

77. What bothers the man about Torland Advertising?

(A) Their failure to meet deadlines
(B) Their problems with staffing
(C) Their request to revise a contract
(D) Their focus on cost cutting

78. What does the man mean when he says, "Here's the thing"?

(A) He will demonstrate a product.
(B) He has forgotten a word.
(C) He has found what he was looking for.
(D) He will introduce a point to consider.

79. What are the listeners asked to look at?

(A) A design idea
(B) A business contract
(C) An advertisement
(D) A budget

※ 此部分文字為錄音內容，不會印在試題本上。

Questions 77 through 79 refer to the following excerpt from a meeting.

So I called this meeting to discuss our contract with Torland Advertising and to decide whether we should … ahm … should continue to use them to develop our radio advertising materials. I had a discussion with their people yesterday and I have to say, I'm a little concerned. They seem much more focused on cutting their costs than they are on providing good quality advertising for us. Here's the thing. If we decide to end this business relationship, we'll need to pay them for anything they've already developed. Please take a minute to look at this contract with me. You'll see that's part of the agreement we made.

解答：77. (D)　78.(D)　79.(B)

Program	
Presenter	**Time**
Ms. Carbajal	1:00–1:50
Mr. Buteux	1:55–2:45
BREAK	2:45–3:00
Mr. Chambers	3:00–3:50
Ms. Ohta	3:55–4:45

80. Where most likely is the speaker?

(A) At an award ceremony
(B) At a musical performance
(C) At a retirement celebration
(D) At a training seminar

81. What are listeners asked to do?

(A) Stay seated during the break
(B) Carry their valuables with them
(C) Return any borrowed equipment
(D) Share printed programs with others

82. Look at the graphic. Who will be the final presenter?

(A) Ms. Carbajal
(B) Mr. Buteux
(C) Mr. Chambers
(D) Ms. Ohta

※ 此部分文字為錄音內容，不會印在試題本上。

Questions 80 through 82 refer to the following talk and program.

We're happy to see you all at this seminar this afternoon—we have a lot of useful information to cover. But before we start, a few administrative details. There will be one break, half way through the afternoon. You can leave your laptops here if you leave the room—there will always be someone in here—but do keep your money and phones or … ah … other small electronic devices with you. Don't leave them at the tables. And please note that there's an error in your printed program: there will be a change—a switch—in times for the last two presenters. Ms. Ohta has to leave a little early today.

解答：80. (D)　81. (B)　82. (C)

聽力測驗
全真試題(1)

In the Listening test, you will be asked to demonstrate how well you understand spoken English. The entire Listening test will last approximately 45 minutes. There are four parts, and directions are given for each part. You must mark your answers on the separate answer sheet. Do not write your answers in your test book.

※ 使用本書模擬測驗時,可利用本書提供之答案卡作答。此張答案卡與正式測驗答案卡相同, 但僅供本書練習作答時使用,非正式測驗答案卡。

LISTENING TEST

In the Listening test, you will be asked to demonstrate how well you understand spoken English. The entire Listening test will last approximately 45 minutes. There are four parts, and directions are given for each part. You must mark your answers on the separate answer sheet. Do not write your answers in your test book.

PART 1

Directions: For each question in this part, you will hear four statements about a picture in your test book. When you hear the statements, you must select the one statement that best describes what you see in the picture. Then find the number of the question on your answer sheet and mark your answer. The statements will not be printed in your test book and will be spoken only one time.

Statement (C), "They're sitting at a table," is the best description of the picture, so you should select answer (C) and mark it on your answer sheet.

1.

2.

GO ON TO THE NEXT PAGE

3.

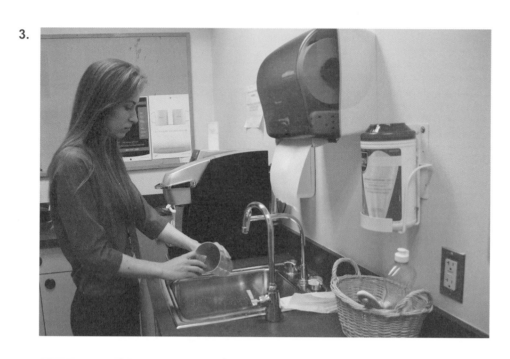

4.

5.

6.

GO ON TO THE NEXT PAGE ➤

PART 2

Directions: You will hear a question or statement and three responses spoken in English. They will not be printed in your test book and will be spoken only one time. Select the best response to the question or statement and mark the letter (A), (B), or (C) on your answer sheet.

7. Mark your answer on your answer sheet.

8. Mark your answer on your answer sheet.

9. Mark your answer on your answer sheet.

10. Mark your answer on your answer sheet.

11. Mark your answer on your answer sheet.

12. Mark your answer on your answer sheet.

13. Mark your answer on your answer sheet.

14. Mark your answer on your answer sheet.

15. Mark your answer on your answer sheet.

16. Mark your answer on your answer sheet.

17. Mark your answer on your answer sheet.

18. Mark your answer on your answer sheet.

19. Mark your answer on your answer sheet.

20. Mark your answer on your answer sheet.

21. Mark your answer on your answer sheet.

22. Mark your answer on your answer sheet.

23. Mark your answer on your answer sheet.

24. Mark your answer on your answer sheet.

25. Mark your answer on your answer sheet.

26. Mark your answer on your answer sheet.

27. Mark your answer on your answer sheet.

28. Mark your answer on your answer sheet.

29. Mark your answer on your answer sheet.

30. Mark your answer on your answer sheet.

31. Mark your answer on your answer sheet.

PART 3

Directions: You will hear some conversations between two or more people. You will be asked to answer three questions about what the speakers say in each conversation. Select the best response to each question and mark the letter (A), (B), (C), or (D) on your answer sheet. The conversations will not be printed in your test book and will be spoken only one time.

32. Where does the conversation most likely take place?

(A) At a library
(B) At a theater
(C) At a museum
(D) At a restaurant

33. What problem does the man mention?

(A) A brochure contains an error.
(B) A shipment is late.
(C) A guest list has been misplaced.
(D) A computer is not working.

34. What will the woman most likely do next?

(A) Contact a coordinator
(B) Submit a work order
(C) Upload some images
(D) Purchase some supplies

35. Who most likely are the speakers?

(A) Cleaners
(B) Servers
(C) Nutritionists
(D) Food critics

36. Why will the man talk to some cooks?

(A) To compliment their work
(B) To ask for some advice
(C) To change an assignment
(D) To update an order

37. What does the man mean when he says, "I have tickets to a baseball game on Thursday"?

(A) He cannot help the woman.
(B) He has similar interests as the woman.
(C) He wants to invite the woman to an event.
(D) He is concerned that tickets will sell out.

38. What type of business do the speakers own?

(A) A grocery store
(B) A moving company
(C) A construction company
(D) An accounting firm

39. What does the man suggest doing?

(A) Extending business hours
(B) Buying new equipment
(C) Hiring more employees
(D) Advertising online

40. What does the woman say she will do?

(A) Review a budget
(B) Consult an expert
(C) Print an inventory list
(D) Check a floor plan

41. Where does the man most likely work?

(A) At a car repair shop
(B) At a manufacturing plant
(C) At a taxi service
(D) At a law office

42. What does the woman ask the man about?

(A) A project deadline
(B) A logo design
(C) The cost of some services
(D) The quality of some materials

43. What does the man say he will give to the woman?

(A) A brochure
(B) A discount
(C) Free delivery
(D) Sample products

GO ON TO THE NEXT PAGE ➡

44. What will take place this year?

   (A) A corporate merger
   (B) A software update
   (C) A research study
   (D) An office relocation

45. What problem does the man mention?

   (A) Some paperwork has been lost.
   (B) Some equipment is broken.
   (C) Some funding was not approved.
   (D) Some designs were rejected.

46. What will the woman do next?

   (A) Revise a budget
   (B) Schedule a meeting
   (C) Find some contact information
   (D) Hire a consultant

47. Where most likely are the speakers?

   (A) At a storage facility
   (B) At an electronics factory
   (C) At a film studio
   (D) At a technology exhibition

48. What problem are the men discussing?

   (A) Some products are defective.
   (B) A container is not large enough.
   (C) There are not enough workers.
   (D) An order was canceled.

49. What does the woman say she will do?

   (A) Offer a discount
   (B) Renegotiate a contract
   (C) Inspect a shipment
   (D) Notify an engineer

50. Where are the speakers?

   (A) At a pharmacy
   (B) At a clothing store
   (C) At a dental clinic
   (D) At a fitness center

51. What does the woman explain to the man?

   (A) He has missed an appointment.
   (B) A price has changed.
   (C) A business is closing soon.
   (D) An item is not available.

52. What does the man say he will do?

   (A) Complete a customer survey
   (B) Return another day
   (C) Look up some data
   (D) Pay with a credit card

53. What type of business does the woman work for?

   (A) A telephone company
   (B) An airline company
   (C) An accounting firm
   (D) A department store

54. What does the man imply when he says, "my bag weighs 30 kilograms"?

   (A) He plans to buy a different bag.
   (B) He needs help carrying his bag.
   (C) His bag does not have any extra space.
   (D) His bag does not meet the requirements.

55. Why is the man in a hurry?

   (A) His flight is about to depart.
   (B) His presentation is starting soon.
   (C) His phone battery is low.
   (D) His taxi is waiting.

56. What does the man confirm that he has received?

    (A) A copy of a contract
    (B) An employee manual
    (C) A security badge
    (D) Some log-in information

57. Where are the speakers going next?

    (A) To an airport
    (B) To a cafeteria
    (C) To a training workshop
    (D) To a client meeting

58. What does the woman say is currently happening at the company?

    (A) A computer system is being upgraded.
    (B) A parking area is being repaired.
    (C) Some policies are being revised.
    (D) Some solar panels are being installed.

59. What field do the speakers most likely work in?

    (A) Engineering
    (B) Accounting
    (C) Education
    (D) Advertising

60. What problem is mentioned?

    (A) A power cord is missing.
    (B) A microphone is not functioning properly.
    (C) A screen is not displaying an image.
    (D) A battery is not charging.

61. What does the woman suggest doing?

    (A) Using a different computer
    (B) Moving to another room
    (C) Postponing a demonstration
    (D) Contacting technical support

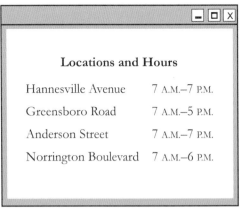

Locations and Hours	
Hannesville Avenue	7 A.M.–7 P.M.
Greensboro Road	7 A.M.–5 P.M.
Anderson Street	7 A.M.–7 P.M.
Norrington Boulevard	7 A.M.–6 P.M.

62. Where does the man work?

    (A) At a furniture store
    (B) At a painting company
    (C) At a bakery
    (D) At a gym

63. What does the woman say is important?

    (A) A healthy option
    (B) A low price
    (C) A fast delivery
    (D) A specific decoration

64. Look at the graphic. Which location did the woman call?

    (A) Hannesville Avenue
    (B) Greensboro Road
    (C) Anderson Street
    (D) Norrington Boulevard

GO ON TO THE NEXT PAGE

65. What is the occasion for the special sale?

(A) A store anniversary
(B) A public holiday
(C) A grand opening
(D) A customer contest

66. Look at the graphic. Which discount will be changed?

(A) 10%
(B) 15%
(C) 25%
(D) 40%

67. What does the woman say she will do tomorrow?

(A) Receive a shipment
(B) Contact a caterer
(C) Go to a printshop
(D) Organize a display

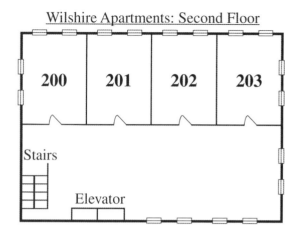

68. Who is the man?

(A) A building manager
(B) A delivery driver
(C) A repair person
(D) An interior decorator

69. What does the woman complain about?

(A) The high cost of a service
(B) The noise outside her apartment
(C) The length of a renovation project
(D) The limited access to parking

70. Look at the graphic. Which apartment does the man mention?

(A) Apartment 200
(B) Apartment 201
(C) Apartment 202
(D) Apartment 203

PART 4

Directions: You will hear some talks given by a single speaker. You will be asked to answer three questions about what the speaker says in each talk. Select the best response to each question and mark the letter (A), (B), (C), or (D) on your answer sheet. The talks will not be printed in your test book and will be spoken only one time.

71. Where are the listeners?

(A) At an airport
(B) At a bus terminal
(C) At a train station
(D) At a taxi stand

72. What does the speaker ask the listeners to do?

(A) Present some identification
(B) Speak with a representative
(C) Provide a credit card number
(D) Weigh some baggage

73. What will the listeners receive as a courtesy?

(A) Hotel accommodations
(B) Complimentary meals
(C) Priority seating
(D) Free Internet service

74. What will be installed this weekend?

(A) Drinking fountains
(B) Videoconferencing equipment
(C) An air-conditioning system
(D) An alarm system

75. According to the speaker, why is the change being made?

(A) To reduce costs
(B) To increase comfort
(C) To boost productivity
(D) To comply with guidelines

76. What should the listeners do before they leave work on Friday?

(A) Talk to their managers
(B) Move their cars
(C) Cover their desks
(D) Complete a questionnaire

77. Why has the speaker arranged the meeting?

(A) To go over sales data
(B) To distribute client information
(C) To give a demonstration
(D) To assign special projects

78. What should the listeners assure clients about?

(A) Orders will be processed on time.
(B) Contracts will be mailed.
(C) Discounts will be applied.
(D) Factory tours will be available.

79. What does the speaker imply when she says, "I had to read through the manual twice"?

(A) A company policy is surprising.
(B) A publication may contain some errors.
(C) A manual was updated.
(D) A software program may be difficult to learn.

80. What is the radio program mainly about?

(A) Technology
(B) Finance
(C) Travel
(D) Fitness

81. According to the speaker, what happened last week?

(A) A company president retired.
(B) A firm celebrated an anniversary.
(C) A mobile application was released.
(D) A new book was published.

82. What will Mr. Orton be discussing?

(A) How he expanded his business
(B) How to make professional contacts
(C) Ways he stays active
(D) Ways to advertise on social media

GO ON TO THE NEXT PAGE

83. What has the company decided to do?

(A) Launch a Web site
(B) Create a new type of beverage
(C) Sell products in vending machines
(D) Advertise in sports magazines

84. What did a survey indicate about customers?

(A) They prefer natural ingredients.
(B) They make online purchases.
(C) They like celebrity promotions.
(D) They want lower prices.

85. What are the listeners asked to do?

(A) Try a sample
(B) Review a proposal
(C) Submit suggestions
(D) Contact some customers

86. What type of event is the speaker discussing?

(A) A health fair
(B) An investment course
(C) A holiday celebration
(D) A restaurant opening

87. Why does the speaker say, "I always park behind the bank"?

(A) To show surprise
(B) To make a complaint
(C) To give a recommendation
(D) To correct a mistake

88. What will the listeners do next?

(A) Look at a map
(B) Watch a film
(C) Update a calendar
(D) Divide into groups

89. What is the speaker shopping for?

(A) Groceries
(B) Kitchen appliances
(C) Sporting goods
(D) Computer accessories

90. What does the speaker mean when he says, "it's pretty far from here"?

(A) He is unable to complete a task today.
(B) He will need to borrow a car.
(C) He may be late for an appointment.
(D) He needs driving directions.

91. What does the speaker ask the listener to do?

(A) Print a document
(B) Address some letters
(C) Arrange an interview
(D) Process a refund

92. What type of products does the speaker review?

(A) Home furniture
(B) Video games
(C) Cosmetics
(D) Exercise clothing

93. Why does the speaker apologize?

(A) A description was incorrect.
(B) A guest has canceled.
(C) A sponsor has withdrawn.
(D) A project has been delayed.

94. What activity did the speaker participate in last week?

(A) A competition
(B) A fashion show
(C) A fund-raiser
(D) A community festival

Kinbridge Farm

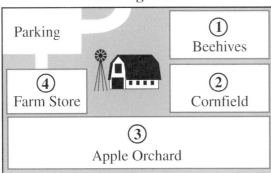

	Mon.	Tues.	Wed.	Thurs.
8:00	Planning meeting			
9:00		Work on budget report	Leadership training	Finish budget report
10:00	Presentation		Directors' strategy meeting	
1:00		Team meeting		

95. Look at the graphic. What area is currently closed?

(A) Area 1
(B) Area 2
(C) Area 3
(D) Area 4

96. According to the speaker, what will the listeners receive?

(A) Homemade cookies
(B) A discount coupon
(C) A bottle of water
(D) Free fruit

97. What does the speaker remind the listeners about?

(A) What equipment to bring
(B) When to return to the parking area
(C) Where to buy some goods
(D) Who sponsored the tour

98. What is the speaker concerned about?

(A) A short timeline
(B) An advertising campaign
(C) Technical issues
(D) Inexperienced staff

99. Look at the graphic. When does the speaker suggest meeting?

(A) On Monday
(B) On Tuesday
(C) On Wednesday
(D) On Thursday

100. What does the speaker ask the listener to do?

(A) Finalize a construction schedule
(B) Review a budget
(C) Create a meeting agenda
(D) Call a potential client

This is the end of the Listening test.

NO TEST MATERIAL ON THIS PAGE

聽力測驗
全真試題(2)

In the Listening test, you will be asked to demonstrate how well you understand spoken English. The entire Listening test will last approximately 45 minutes. There are four parts, and directions are given for each part. You must mark your answers on the separate answer sheet. Do not write your answers in your test book.

※ 使用本書模擬測驗時，可利用本書提供之答案卡作答。此張答案卡與正式測驗答案卡相同，但僅供本書練習作答時使用，非正式測驗答案卡。

LISTENING TEST

In the Listening test, you will be asked to demonstrate how well you understand spoken English. The entire Listening test will last approximately 45 minutes. There are four parts, and directions are given for each part. You must mark your answers on the separate answer sheet. Do not write your answers in your test book.

PART 1

Directions: For each question in this part, you will hear four statements about a picture in your test book. When you hear the statements, you must select the one statement that best describes what you see in the picture. Then find the number of the question on your answer sheet and mark your answer. The statements will not be printed in your test book and will be spoken only one time.

Statement (C), "They're sitting at a table," is the best description of the picture, so you should select answer (C) and mark it on your answer sheet.

1.

2.

GO ON TO THE NEXT PAGE

3.

4.

5.

6.

GO ON TO THE NEXT PAGE

PART 2

Directions: You will hear a question or statement and three responses spoken in English. They will not be printed in your test book and will be spoken only one time. Select the best response to the question or statement and mark the letter (A), (B), or (C) on your answer sheet.

7. Mark your answer on your answer sheet.

8. Mark your answer on your answer sheet.

9. Mark your answer on your answer sheet.

10. Mark your answer on your answer sheet.

11. Mark your answer on your answer sheet.

12. Mark your answer on your answer sheet.

13. Mark your answer on your answer sheet.

14. Mark your answer on your answer sheet.

15. Mark your answer on your answer sheet.

16. Mark your answer on your answer sheet.

17. Mark your answer on your answer sheet.

18. Mark your answer on your answer sheet.

19. Mark your answer on your answer sheet.

20. Mark your answer on your answer sheet.

21. Mark your answer on your answer sheet.

22. Mark your answer on your answer sheet.

23. Mark your answer on your answer sheet.

24. Mark your answer on your answer sheet.

25. Mark your answer on your answer sheet.

26. Mark your answer on your answer sheet.

27. Mark your answer on your answer sheet.

28. Mark your answer on your answer sheet.

29. Mark your answer on your answer sheet.

30. Mark your answer on your answer sheet.

31. Mark your answer on your answer sheet.

PART 3

Directions: You will hear some conversations between two or more people. You will be asked to answer three questions about what the speakers say in each conversation. Select the best response to each question and mark the letter (A), (B), (C), or (D) on your answer sheet. The conversations will not be printed in your test book and will be spoken only one time.

TEST 2

32. Where are the speakers?

(A) At a supermarket
(B) At a furniture store
(C) At a clothing retailer
(D) At an automobile repair shop

33. Why does Tom ask the woman for help?

(A) A receipt is missing.
(B) A computer is broken.
(C) A warranty is expired.
(D) An item is out of stock.

34. What does the woman offer to do for the customer?

(A) Give him in-store credit
(B) Check a storage room
(C) Call another store
(D) Provide express delivery service

35. Why is the man calling?

(A) To inquire about a job
(B) To request a prescription
(C) To ask about business hours
(D) To reschedule an appointment

36. What does the woman say about Dr. Ramirez?

(A) She is presenting at a conference next week.
(B) She works at two different locations.
(C) She teaches at a medical school.
(D) She usually does not work on Wednesdays.

37. What does the woman give to the man?

(A) Directions to a medical center
(B) A Web site address
(C) A phone number
(D) A cost estimate

38. Who most likely is the woman?

(A) A library employee
(B) A professor
(C) A café owner
(D) A museum curator

39. What event will take place next weekend?

(A) A film screening
(B) An academic lecture
(C) A musical performance
(D) An art show

40. What will the event's profits be used for?

(A) Purchasing new merchandise
(B) Offering an internship
(C) Creating a tutoring program
(D) Renovating part of a building

41. Where is the woman?

(A) At a hotel
(B) At an airport
(C) At a car rental office
(D) At a train station

42. According to the man, what has caused a delay?

(A) Road construction
(B) Bad weather
(C) A scheduling mistake
(D) A mechanical problem

43. What does the man say he will do?

(A) Contact his supervisor
(B) Issue a boarding pass
(C) Apply a discount
(D) Print a map

GO ON TO THE NEXT PAGE

44. Which department does the woman work in?

(A) Marketing
(B) Accounting
(C) Product development
(D) Human resources

45. What does the woman mean when she says, "I don't have anything scheduled that day"?

(A) She did not receive an invitation.
(B) She has finished interviewing candidates.
(C) She wants to revise a travel itinerary.
(D) She can give a presentation.

46. What will the man send to the woman?

(A) An agenda
(B) A manual
(C) A résumé
(D) A feedback form

---

47. Who is Theodore?

(A) An architect
(B) A real estate agent
(C) A graphic designer
(D) A journalist

48. What does Theodore say he did?

(A) He scheduled a meeting.
(B) He took some photographs.
(C) He e-mailed a document.
(D) He visited a construction site.

49. What does the woman want to discuss?

(A) A staffing change
(B) A timeline
(C) A technical problem
(D) A budget

---

50. Where does the woman want to work?

(A) At a factory
(B) At a restaurant
(C) At a fitness center
(D) At a clothing store

51. Why did the woman leave her previous job?

(A) She began university studies.
(B) Her commute was too long.
(C) The company closed.
(D) The pay was low.

52. What does the man explain to the woman?

(A) There are evening shifts.
(B) A uniform will be provided.
(C) Training will be necessary.
(D) The company is very small.

---

53. What does the woman ask the man to do?

(A) Review an order
(B) Set up a computer
(C) Organize a conference
(D) Contact a client

54. What will the man bring to the woman?

(A) A catalog
(B) A calendar
(C) A list of suppliers
(D) A building directory

55. What does the woman plan to do next week?

(A) Send out a newsletter
(B) Sign a contract
(C) Go on a trip
(D) Submit some slides

---

56. What are the speakers mainly discussing?

    (A) A focus group
    (B) Computer-use policies
    (C) An upcoming merger
    (D) Employee rewards

57. What does the man imply when he says, "You spend more time with your team than I do"?

    (A) The woman's team requires more staff.
    (B) The woman should schedule fewer meetings.
    (C) The woman is the best person to decide.
    (D) The woman should have noticed a mistake.

58. What does the man advise the woman to do next?

    (A) Speak with a colleague
    (B) Research a competitor
    (C) Download an application
    (D) Attend a seminar

59. What is being discussed?

    (A) Appliances
    (B) Some software
    (C) Printers
    (D) Television sets

60. What did the man recently do?

    (A) He received a certificate.
    (B) He published a book.
    (C) He started a business.
    (D) He renovated an office.

61. What does the woman say is available?

    (A) Overnight shipping
    (B) An extended warranty
    (C) An online user manual
    (D) A free trial

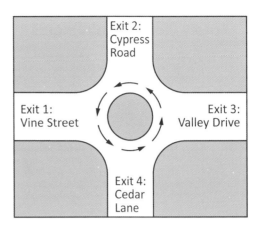

62. What event are the speakers going to attend?

    (A) A concert
    (B) A marathon
    (C) An art show
    (D) A restaurant festival

63. Who most likely are the speakers?

    (A) Chefs
    (B) Musicians
    (C) Investors
    (D) Journalists

64. Look at the graphic. Which road will the speakers take next?

    (A) Vine Street
    (B) Cypress Road
    (C) Valley Drive
    (D) Cedar Lane

GO ON TO THE NEXT PAGE

Safety Gear Requirements				
	Goggles	Ear protection	Hard hat	Foot protection
Factory floor		X		
Packaging room	X			
Loading dock				X
Supply room			X	

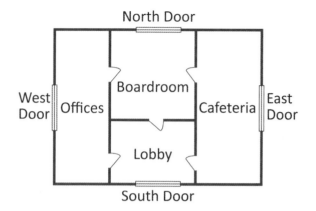

65. Why is the woman visiting the man's factory?

(A) To learn about management strategies
(B) To inspect some equipment
(C) To train new employees
(D) To enact a new guideline

66. What reason does the man give for his results?

(A) Hiring outside consultants
(B) Building relationships with staff
(C) Investing in the most recent technology
(D) Maintaining diverse suppliers

67. Look at the graphic. What safety gear does the woman need to wear?

(A) Goggles
(B) Ear protection
(C) A hard hat
(D) Foot protection

68. What most likely is the woman's job title?

(A) Custodian
(B) Locksmith
(C) Landscaper
(D) Parking attendant

69. Look at the graphic. Which door are the speakers discussing?

(A) The North Door
(B) The East Door
(C) The South Door
(D) The West Door

70. What does the man remind the woman to do?

(A) Display her badge
(B) Store her belongings
(C) Submit her time sheet
(D) Validate her parking pass

PART 4

Directions: You will hear some talks given by a single speaker. You will be asked to answer three questions about what the speaker says in each talk. Select the best response to each question and mark the letter (A), (B), (C), or (D) on your answer sheet. The talks will not be printed in your test book and will be spoken only one time.

71. What is the news report mainly about?

    (A) A museum exhibit
    (B) A holiday parade
    (C) A building renovation
    (D) A sports competition

72. Who is Byron Lang?

    (A) A travel agent
    (B) An architect
    (C) A city official
    (D) An athlete

73. What does the speaker say will be provided next year?

    (A) Extra parking
    (B) Weekend tours
    (C) Souvenirs
    (D) Job opportunities

74. What product is the speaker discussing?

    (A) An electric car
    (B) A mobile phone
    (C) A washing machine
    (D) A refrigerator

75. Why does the speaker say a product is unique?

    (A) It is the smallest model available.
    (B) It is the least expensive model available.
    (C) Its motor is very quiet.
    (D) Its battery charges quickly.

76. What does the speaker say the listeners can do?

    (A) Put their names on a waiting list
    (B) Submit their reviews online
    (C) Participate in a product demonstration
    (D) Assemble an item independently

77. What is the speaker planning for next week?

    (A) An awards ceremony
    (B) A poetry reading
    (C) A gardening lecture
    (D) A glassmaking workshop

78. What does the speaker say she sent to the listener?

    (A) An outline
    (B) A credit card number
    (C) A pamphlet
    (D) A coupon

79. Why does the speaker say, "but we're also available on Tuesday"?

    (A) To ask for a budget increase
    (B) To confirm attendance
    (C) To complain about a scheduling conflict
    (D) To suggest holding an additional class

80. What type of business created the tutorial?

    (A) A post office
    (B) A community college
    (C) An electronics company
    (D) A paper goods manufacturer

81. According to the speaker, what should the listeners print out?

    (A) A shipping label
    (B) A manual
    (C) An invoice
    (D) Installation directions

82. What does the speaker offer to the listeners?

    (A) A warranty
    (B) A discount
    (C) Free accessories
    (D) Express delivery

GO ON TO THE NEXT PAGE

83. What department does the speaker work in?

(A) Accounting
(B) Legal
(C) Security
(D) Human Resources

84. What does the speaker say the listeners need permission to do?

(A) Meet in a designated area
(B) Remove work documents
(C) Bring guests into the building
(D) Sign client contracts

85. What change does the speaker mention?

(A) Doors will now be locked.
(B) Management groups will be reorganized.
(C) A cafeteria will offer breakfast.
(D) A computer system will be upgraded.

---

86. What type of business does the speaker work in?

(A) Automobile sales
(B) Interior design
(C) Food distribution
(D) Paper manufacturing

87. According to the survey results, what do customers like about the speaker's company?

(A) The quality of its products
(B) The location of its branches
(C) Its dedication to customer satisfaction
(D) Its innovative advertisements

88. What does the speaker imply when he says, "You're familiar with Fox International Deliveries, aren't you"?

(A) He wants to change service providers.
(B) He wants the listener to give a presentation.
(C) He wants to promote the listener to a new role.
(D) He wants to merge with another company.

---

89. What can the listeners receive at no cost?

(A) Parking
(B) Beverages
(C) Internet access
(D) Extra space

90. What does the speaker imply when he says, "train tickets are expensive"?

(A) The listeners should not take the train.
(B) The listeners should not attend an event.
(C) The listeners should obtain approval for an expense.
(D) The listeners should travel in another season.

91. Why are the listeners encouraged to visit a Web site?

(A) To apply for funding
(B) To receive a reduced price
(C) To fill out a survey
(D) To submit a form

---

92. What industry does the speaker work in?

(A) Electronics
(B) Finance
(C) Marketing
(D) Tourism

93. How does the speaker say she stays informed about current trends?

(A) She follows social networking sites.
(B) She analyzes consumer reviews.
(C) She reads industry journals.
(D) She interviews movie stars.

94. What does the speaker suggest changing?

(A) Where to open a new office
(B) When to sell certain products
(C) How to arrange a display
(D) What brands to carry

SANCHEZ' CATERING COMPANY
MENU

	MEDIUM	LARGE
MEAT PLATTER	$300	$500
VEGETABLE PLATTER	$250	$400

95. What event is the speaker planning?

(A) A board meeting
(B) A retirement party
(C) A graduation party
(D) A job fair

96. Look at the graphic. How much will the speaker pay for his food order?

(A) $250
(B) $300
(C) $400
(D) $500

97. What does the speaker ask about?

(A) Whether he is eligible for a discount
(B) When food servers will arrive
(C) Which serving utensils are included
(D) Whether food containers must be returned

LEBBINSVILLE AMUSEMENT PARK
Grand Opening: August 12

Special Events All Summer!

Wednesdays	Comedy Special
Thursdays	Magic Show
Fridays	Music Performance
Saturdays	Parade

98. Who most likely is the speaker?

(A) A park owner
(B) A journalist
(C) An electrician
(D) A graphic designer

99. Look at the graphic. Which special event was canceled?

(A) The Comedy Special
(B) The Magic Show
(C) The Music Performance
(D) The Parade

100. What will the speaker do this afternoon?

(A) Introduce a guest
(B) Show a video
(C) Describe a contest
(D) Make a phone call

This is the end of the Listening test.

NO TEST MATERIAL ON THIS PAGE

試題解答與
分數及目標能力計算

1. 本書所提供的分數換算方式，僅適用於 *ETS*® 所提供的全真模擬試題，與實際
   測驗的成績計算方法不同，故本書獲得的分數為參考分數。

2. 本書為《*TOEIC*® 聽力與閱讀測驗官方全真試題指南 Vol.8 聽力篇》，僅能計算
   聽力測驗之參考分數；若想了解閱讀測驗之參考分數，請使用《*TOEIC*® 聽力
   與閱讀測驗官方全真試題指南 Vol.8 閱讀篇》。

全真試題 (1) 解答及目標能力對應表

PART 1

題號	正解	目標能力①	②	③	④	⑤
1	B	●				
2	A		●			
3	D	●				
4	C		●			
5	D		●			
6	A		●			

PART 2

題號	正解	目標能力①	②	③	④	⑤
7	C		●			
8	B		●			
9	A		●			
10	A		●			
11	C		●			
12	B		●			
13	A		●			
14	C		●			
15	A				●	
16	B				●	
17	C			●		
18	A	●			●	
19	C		●			
20	C		●			
21	A	●			●	
22	A	●			●	
23	C	●				
24	B	●			●	
25	B	●			●	
26	A	●				
27	A	●			●	
28	C			●		
29	B	●				
30	B	●			●	
31	A	●			●	

PART 3

題號	正解	目標能力①	②	③	④	⑤
32	C		●			
33	B			●		
34	C			●		
35	B	●				
36	D			●		
37	A	●				●
38	A			●		
39	B			●		
40	D			●		
41	A	●				
42	C			●		
43	A			●		
44	A			●		
45	D			●		
46	B			●		
47	B	●				
48	A	●				
49	D			●		
50	A			●		
51	D			●		
52	B			●		
53	B	●				
54	D	●				●
55	C			●		
56	C			●		
57	B			●		
58	D			●		
59	D	●				
60	B			●		
61	A			●		
62	C			●		
63	D			●		
64	B			●		
65	C	●				
66	D			●		
67	C			●		
68	A			●		
69	B			●		
70	D			●		

PART 4

題號	正解	目標能力①	②	③	④	⑤
71	A	●				
72	B			●		
73	A			●		
74	C			●		
75	B			●		
76	C			●		
77	C			●		
78	B			●		
79	D	●				●
80	B	●				
81	D			●		
82	A			●		
83	B			●		
84	A			●		
85	C			●		
86	A	●				●
87	C	●				●
88	D			●		
89	D	●				
90	A	●				●
91	C			●		
92	D			●		
93	D			●		
94	A			●		
95	B			●		
96	D			●		
97	C			●		
98	D			●		
99	C			●		
100	B			●		

●●●●● 詳細目標能力對應請參考第 55 頁

全真試題 (2) 解答及目標能力對應表

詳細目標能力對應請參考第 55 頁

PART 1

題號	正解
1	C
2	D
3	A
4	B
5	B
6	D

PART 2

題號	正解
7	C
8	C
9	B
10	A
11	B
12	B
13	A
14	C
15	B
16	A
17	C
18	A
19	B
20	B
21	C
22	B
23	A
24	A
25	C
26	C
27	A
28	C
29	B
30	B
31	C

PART 3

題號	正解
32	B
33	A
34	A
35	D
36	B
37	C
38	A
39	D
40	C
41	B
42	A
43	C
44	B
45	D
46	A
47	B
48	C
49	B
50	D
51	B
52	C
53	A
54	A
55	C
56	D
57	C
58	A
59	B
60	C
61	D
62	D
63	D
64	C
65	A
66	B
67	C
68	B
69	B
70	A

PART 4

題號	正解
71	C
72	B
73	B
74	A
75	D
76	A
77	D
78	A
79	D
80	C
81	A
82	B
83	C
84	B
85	A
86	D
87	C
88	A
89	C
90	A
91	B
92	C
93	A
94	B
95	C
96	D
97	B
98	A
99	A
100	D

分數計算方式

找出原始分數		對應出量尺分數範圍

找出原始分數

請參考「試題解答及目標能力對應表」，對應出聽力測驗的答對題數，即為原始分數。

對應出量尺分數範圍

根據下方的「分數換算表」，找到原始對應的量尺分數範圍。

Step 1

Step 2

範例：答對的題數為 35 題，原始分數為 35 分，對應出量尺分數範圍為 105-175 分。

聽力測驗分數換算表			
原始分數範圍	量尺分數範圍	原始分數範圍	量尺分數範圍
96 − 100	475 − 495	41 − 45	155 − 230
91 − 95	435 − 495	36 − 40	125 − 205
86 − 90	405 − 475	31 − 35	105 − 175
81 − 85	370 − 450	26 − 30	85 − 145
76 − 80	345 − 420	21 − 25	60 − 115
71 − 75	320 − 390	16 − 20	30 − 90
66 − 70	290 − 360	11 − 15	5 − 70
61 − 65	265 − 335	6 − 10	5 − 60
56 − 60	235 − 310	1 − 5	5 − 50
51 − 55	210 − 280	0	5 − 35
46 − 50	180 − 255		

目標能力正答率計算方式

<table>
<tr>
<td>

對應相同目標能力的答對題目

- 請參考「試題解答及目標能力對應表」，對應出聽力測驗各項目標能力之答對題數。
- 某些題目有兩項目標能力，計算答對題數時，同一題應重複加總。例如：全真試題 (1) 第18題答對，則在計算綠色目標能力答對題數時計算一次；而在計算紫色目標能力答對題數時，也需再納入計算一次。

Step 1

</td>
<td>

計算各目標能力的答對比例

$$\frac{\text{該目標能力答對題數}}{\text{相同目標能力之總題數}} \times 100\%$$

Step 2

</td>
</tr>
</table>

範例：目標能力 Can understand details in short spoken texts 的題數在全真試題 (1) 中共有 16 題，應試者答對了其中 8 題，套入計算公式 $\frac{8}{16}$ x 100%，則該目標能力之正答率為 50%。

目標能力對應

- Can infer gist, purpose and basic context based on information that is explicitly stated in short spoken texts
- Can infer gist, purpose and basic context based on information that is explicitly stated in extended spoken texts
- Can understand details in short spoken texts
- Can understand details in extended spoken texts
- Can understand a speaker's purpose or implied meaning in a phrase or sentence

中文翻譯及
目標能力解析

題目／中文翻譯

---

1. Can infer gist, purpose and basic context based on information that is explicitly stated in short spoken texts

(A) He's watering some flowers.
(B) He's talking on a phone.
(C) He's drinking from a coffee mug.
(D) He's tying his shoe.

(A) 他正在澆花。
(B) 他正在講電話。
(C) 他正在用咖啡杯喝東西。
(D) 他正在綁他的鞋帶。

重點解說

正解 (B)

男子拿著手機正在講電話。talk on a phone「講電話」。
(A) 男子身旁有個花盆，但他手裡沒有澆水壺，且他也沒有在澆花。water some flowers「澆花」。
(C) 男子右腳旁有咖啡杯，但他沒有拿著杯子在飲用。coffee mug「咖啡杯」，drinking「飲用」。
(D) 男子沒有在綁鞋帶。tie the shoe「綁鞋帶」，tying 是 tie 的現在進行式。

💡 應試者能理解圖片中人物的動作和物品的單字，從中將正確的語句與圖片配對。

---

2. Can understand details in short spoken texts

(A) One of the men is holding a briefcase.
(B) One of the men is taking off his sunglasses.
(C) They're handing out some flyers.
(D) They're replacing bricks on a pathway.

(A) 其中一個男人正拿著公事包。
(B) 其中一個男人正拿下他的太陽眼鏡。
(C) 他們正在發送傳單。
(D) 他們正在更換人行道的磚塊。

重點解說

正解 (A)

圖片中右邊的男子手裡拿著公事包，故選項 (A) 敘述最合適。briefcase「公事包」。
(B) 右邊男子戴著墨鏡，左邊男子則沒有，且兩人皆沒有正在將墨鏡摘下的動作。take off「拿下」。
(C) 兩名男子手裡都沒有傳單，路上也沒有人接受傳單，可看出他們沒有在發送傳單。hand out「發送」，flyer「傳單」。
(D) 兩名男子站在人行道上，但沒有在替換磚塊。replace「替換」，brick「磚塊」，pathway「人行道」。

💡 應試者能理解動作和物品的單字，並配對圖片，如 (A) 和 (B) 中使之不定代名詞 one of，與 (C) 及 (D) 之單字。

3. Can infer gist, purpose and basic context based on information that is explicitly stated in short spoken texts

(A) She's drying her hands with a paper towel.
(B) She's plugging in an appliance.
(C) She's wiping off a countertop.
(D) She's washing a cup in the sink.

(A) 她正在用紙巾擦乾她的雙手。
(B) 她正在為電器用品插上插頭。
(C) 她正在擦拭流理台。
(D) 她正在洗碗槽內清洗杯子。

重點解說

正解 (D)

圖片中的女子手裡拿著杯子，在水龍頭下方、水槽上方清洗杯子，故選項 (D) 敘述最合適。sink「洗碗槽」。

(A) 在女子的面前有擦手紙，但她正在洗杯子而非擦乾雙手。dry her hands「擦乾雙手」，paper towel「擦手紙」。

(B) 女子沒有插上任何電器用品的插頭。plug in「插上」，appliance「電器用品」。

(C) 女子沒有在擦拭流理台。wipe off「擦拭」，countertop「流理台」。

💡 應試者能理解圖片中人物的動作和物品的單字，需從中將正確的語句與圖片配對。

4. Can understand details in short spoken texts

(A) Leaves are being raked into piles.
(B) Lampposts are being installed near a street.
(C) Benches are positioned along a walkway.
(D) Bicycles are chained to a fence.

(A) 樹葉被耙成一堆。
(B) 街道附近有安裝燈柱。
(C) 沿著人行道有設置長椅。
(D) 腳踏車被拴在圍籬上。

重點解說

正解 (C)

圖片中的長椅都沿著人行道設置。bench「長椅」，position「設置」，walkway「人行道」。

(A) 葉子是鋪平的狀態，並沒有被耙成一堆。leaves「葉子」，leaves 為 leaf 的複數，pile「一堆」。

(B) 街燈是被安裝在人行道旁而非街道旁。在圖中沒有看到街道，且沒有看到安裝工程在進行。lamppost「街燈」，install「安裝」。

(D) 圖片中沒有看到任何一台腳踏車被拴在圍籬上。chain「拴」，fence「圍籬」。

💡 應試者能理解圖片及選項中所提到的物品及相關動作的單字，本題四個選項皆使用被動語法（be 動詞＋過去分詞），應試者需能將選項與圖片配對。

題目/中文翻譯

5. Can understand details in short spoken texts

(A) People are placing suitcases in a vehicle.
(B) People are planting trees in a park.
(C) Cars are being driven down a road.
(D) Tents are being set up in a field.

(A) 人們正把手提箱放到車內。
(B) 人們正在公園裡種樹。
(C) 汽車正在路上行駛。
(D) 空地上正在搭建帳篷。

重點解說

正解 (D)
人們正在空地搭建帳棚。tent「帳棚」，set up「搭建」，field「空地」。
(A) 雖然空地上停有車子，但人們並未將行李箱放入車內。place「放入」，suitcase「行李箱」，vehicle「車子」。
(B) 人們並未在公園裡種樹。plant「栽種」。
(C) 車子並未被開上路。drive down a road「開上路」，driven 是 drive 的過去分詞。

💡 應試者能理解圖片及選項中所提到的動作和物品的單字，選項使用被動語法（be 動詞＋過去分詞），應試者需能將選項與圖片配對。

6. Can understand details in short spoken texts

(A) Lockers are lined up in a hallway.
(B) Shelves are being put up next to a door.
(C) Tiles are being removed from the floor.
(D) Bags have been hung from hooks.

(A) 置物櫃在走廊上排成一排。
(B) 貨架被放在門旁邊。
(C) 地板上的磁磚正在被移除。
(D) 包包掛在鉤子上。

重點解說

正解 (A)
有一排的置物櫃整齊排列在走廊上。locker「置物櫃」，line up「排列」，hallway「走廊」。
(B) 圖中是置物櫃而非貨架。shelf「貨架」（shelf 為單數，shelves 為複數），put up「設置、搭建」。
(C) 磁磚沒有被移除。tile「磁磚」，remove「移除」。
(D) 女子只有拿著一個包包，並非很多個；此外也不確定女子是否將包包掛在鉤子上。hang「掛」（hung 是 hang 的過去式），hook「掛鉤」。

💡 應試者能理解圖片及選項中所提到的動作和物品的單字，選項使用被動語法（be 動詞＋過去分詞），應試者需能將選項與圖片配對。

題 目 / 中 文 翻 譯

7. Can understand details in short spoken texts

Which desk is mine?

(A) At noon on Wednesday.
(B) My computer works.
(C) The one next to the printer.

哪一張桌子是我的？

(A) 在週三中午。
(B) 我的電腦能運作。
(C) 在印表機旁邊的那張（桌子）。

> **正解 (C)**
>
> 重點解說
>
> 「Which...?」詢問哪一張桌子是我的，選項 (C) 具體描述桌子的位置是在印表機旁邊，故為正解。the one 指的是題目所問的桌子。mine 是所有格代名詞，指的是 my desk，使用所有格代名詞是為了使句子不會過於冗長。next to「旁邊」，printer「印表機」。
> (A) 題目並未詢問時間。
> (B) 題目並未詢問電腦狀態是否可以使用。
>
> 💡 應試者能理解問題內容，推論答句之所有格代名詞所稱，才能選出適當的回應。

8. Can understand details in short spoken texts

When does the revenue report come out?

(A) Several policies.
(B) At the end of the quarter.
(C) A local reporter.

營收報告何時公布？

(A) 有許多項政策。
(B) 在這個季末。
(C) 一位當地的記者。

> **正解 (B)**
>
> 重點解說
>
> 「When...?」詢問營收報告何時公布，選項 (B) 描述明確時間點是在季度結束時，故為正解。revenue「營收」，come out「公布」，quarter「季度」。
> (A) 題目並未詢問政策／策略的數量。policy「政策、策略」，policies 為 policy 的複數。
> (C) 當地的記者是一名人物，但題目並未詢問是誰公布報告。local「當地的」，reporter「記者」。
>
> 💡 應試者能理解問題及選項內容，猜測較難的單字可能意思，才能選出適當的回應。

9. Can understand details in short spoken texts

Aren't you assigned to the Robinson account?

(A) Yes, Julie and I are.
(B) Two to three P.M.
(C) The stop sign there.

你不是被指派負責 Robinson 那個客戶嗎？

(A) 是的，Julie 和我。
(B) 下午兩點到三點。
(C) 停車標示那裡。

> **正解 (A)**
>
> 重點解說
>
> 否定句的被動語態（be 動詞＋過去分詞）詢問「你不是被指派負責 Robinson 那個客戶嗎？」。通常 be 動詞開頭的問句要用 Yes／No 回答，此類問句為封閉式問句（Yes／No 問句）；而與之相對的為開放式問句（以 who、what、why 作為開頭）。assign「指派」，account「客戶」。
> (B) 並未詢問時間。
> (C) 表達停車標示的位置，但題目並未詢問標示或位置。stop sign「停車標示」。
>
> 💡 此題問句使用了否定問句，應試者能理解此種句法及選項內容，才能選出適當的回應。

10. Can understand details in short spoken texts

Where can I find the vice president's office?

(A) It's on the second floor.
(B) The filing cabinet on the left.
(C) We have to use official stationery.

副總經理的辦公室在哪裡？

(A) 在二樓。
(B) 在左邊的文件櫃。
(C) 我們必須使用官方的文具。

> **重點解說**
>
> 正解 (A)
>
> 「Where...?」詢問副總經理的辦公室，選項 (A) 具體說出位置「在二樓」，故為正解。vice president「副總經理」。
> (B) 說明文件櫃而非副總經理辦公室的位置。filing cabinet「文件櫃」。
> (C) 題目詢問位置，回答官方文具為答非所問。have to「必須」，official「官方的、正式的」，stationery「文具」。
>
> 💡 應試者能理解題目及選項的單字，才能選出適當的回應。

11. Can understand details in short spoken texts

Who attended the trade show last year?

(A) Nearly half past six.
(B) Sure, we can share a car.
(C) The sales team.

誰參加了去年的貿易展覽會？

(A) 將近六點半。
(B) 當然，我們可以共乘一輛車。
(C) 銷售團隊。

> **重點解說**
>
> 正解 (C)
>
> 「Who...?」詢問誰參與貿易展覽會，選項 (C) 回答 sales team「業務團隊」，故為正解。attend「參與」，trade show「貿易展覽會」。
> (A) 表示時間，nearly「幾乎」，half past six「六點半」，與題目無關。
> (B) 並未提到共乘車輛，答非所問。此回答較會用於針對當前或未來的行動給予建議，加上題目提及 last year，故此選項也不符合題目的時態。
>
> 💡 應試者能理解題目及選項的句法及單字，才能選出最適切的答案。

12. Can understand details in short spoken texts

This is your first visit to this location, right?

(A) Check the parking area.
(B) No, I've been here before.
(C) We won first prize!

這是你第一次拜訪這個地點，對嗎？

(A) 檢查一下停車區域。
(B) 不，我曾經到過這裡。
(C) 我們贏得了第一名。

> **重點解說**
>
> 正解 (B)
>
> 題目用「..., right?」附加問句來與對方確認是否第一次來到此地，選項 (B) 用現在完成式（has／have ＋過去分詞）表達曾經來過，故為正解。
> (A) 此回應為祈使句，不是作為答句。停車區與題目無關，答非所問。parking area「停車區」。
> (C) 題目並未提到獎項，該選項答非所問。won 為 win「贏」的過去式，prize「獎項」。
>
> 💡 應試者能理解附加問句及現在完成式的句法，其中以現在完成式表達曾有之經驗，此為較難的句法。

13. `Can understand details in short spoken texts`

How did the focus group respond to our new logo?

(A) They liked it.
(B) How can I focus this camera?
(C) It's about four thirty.

焦點團體對我們新的商標有什麼反應？

(A) 他們喜歡它（新商標）。
(B) 這台相機該如何對焦？
(C) 大約四點半。

正解 (A)

重點解說

「How...?」詢問焦點團體對於新商標的反應如何。選項 (A) 描述群眾的反應，表示喜歡新商標，故為正解。focus group「焦點團體」，logo「商標」，respond「反應」。
(B) 題目中有提及 focus，但此處為「鏡頭對焦」，與題目無關。
(C) 並未詢問時間。

💡 應試者能理解題目及選項的句法及單字，才能選出最適切的答案。

14. `Can understand details in short spoken texts`

Did you arrange to have the door repaired?

(A) I bought a pair of scissors.
(B) A range of quarterly data.
(C) Yes, I put in a request yesterday.

你安排修繕這道門了嗎？

(A) 我買了一把剪刀。
(B) 一系列的季度數據。
(C) 是的，我昨天提出申請了。

正解 (C)

重點解說

通常以過去式助動詞開頭之疑問句「Did you...?」，須以 Yes／No 回答。題目詢問是否有安排修理門。選項 (C) 除了以 yes 開頭，也說明昨天有送出申請，故為正解。arrange「安排」，repair「修理」，put in a request「送出申請」。
(A) 並未詢問對方買什麼。bought 是 buy「買」的過去式，a pair of「一把」，scissors「剪刀」。
(B) 並未詢問有關數據的訊息。quarterly「每季的」，data「數據」。

💡 應試者能理解題目及選項的句法及單字，才能選出最適切的答案。

15. `Can understand a speaker's purpose or implied meaning in a phrase or sentence`

Would you like to come to dinner with us later tonight?

(A) I'm leading a workshop early tomorrow morning.
(B) The farmers market sells them.
(C) We'll find you a table in the back.

今晚晚一點你想要過來和我們一起吃晚餐嗎？

(A) 明天一大早我要主持一場工作坊。
(B) 農夫市集有在販售。
(C) 我們會在後面幫你找一張桌子。

正解 (A)

重點解說

「Would you like...?」詢問對方今晚是否有意一起吃晚餐，選項 (A) 雖然沒有直接回答 Yes／No，但從回覆「明早要主持一場工作坊」暗指回答者今晚可能無法參與，符合語意。
(B) 題目並未提到農夫市集，答非所問。farmer market「農夫市集」。
(C) 提到 table 雖看似與用餐相關，但問題是詢問對方意願，而非討論餐廳座位位置。

💡 根據題目所示，有時選項的答案不一定會直接回答問題，應試者能理解問題的目的及選項中的句法和單字，才能選出最適切的答案。

16. Can understand a speaker's purpose or implied meaning in a phrase or sentence

When do we launch the mobile phone application?

(A) I'm afraid I just ate.

(B) We're a bit behind schedule.

(C) Because I interviewed her previously.

我們什麼時候發布手機應用程式？

(A) 很抱歉我剛才已經吃過了。

(B) 我們進度有一點落後。

(C) 因為我之前有面試過她了。

重點解說

正解 (B)

「When...?」詢問手機應用程式何時發布。選項 (B) a bit behind schedule「進度有點落後」說明進度，故為正解。launch「發布」，application「應用程式」。

(A) 題目並未詢問有關吃飯的問題。afraid「抱歉、恐怕（委婉地告知不好的消息或提出異議）」。

(C) 題目並未提到面試相關問題。previously「之前」。

💡 有時選項的答案並不一定直接回答問題或不容易看出與問題有關聯，應試者能理解問題的目的及選項中的句法和單字，才能選出最適切的答案。

17. Can understand details in short spoken texts

Have you paid the caterer for the award ceremony yet?

(A) It's a small trophy.

(B) I'd love to go, thanks.

(C) Yes, with the company card.

你付錢給負責頒獎典禮的外燴業者了嗎？

(A) 這是一個小的獎盃。

(B) 我很願意去，謝謝。

(C) 是的，用公司卡。

重點解說

正解 (C)

通常以助動詞「Have you...?」為開頭的問句，要用 Yes／No 回答。題目詢問是否已付錢給負責頒獎典禮的外燴業者，選項 (C) 除了以 yes 為開頭回答，也接續說明是以公司卡付款，符合語意，故為正解。caterer「外燴業者」，award ceremony「頒獎典禮」。

(A) 題目並未詢問獎項內容。trophy「獎盃、獎牌」。

(B) 在表達意願，答非所問。

💡 應試者能理解題目及選項的句法及單字，才能選出最適切的答案。

18. Can infer gist, purpose and basic context based on information that is explicitly stated in short spoken texts

Can understand a speaker's purpose or implied meaning in a phrase or sentence

Why has our supplier increased the delivery cost?

(A) I'll give them a call.

(B) Sure, next week.

(C) How many would you like?

為什麼我們的供應商調漲了運輸費用？

(A) 我會打電話問他們。

(B) 當然，下週。

(C) 你想要多少個？

重點解說

正解 (A)

「Why...?」詢問供應商調漲運輸費用的原因，選項 (A) 說明將會致電給對方，雖然這沒有直接回應問題，但間接表明回答者不清楚原因並將致電對方詢問清楚。give someone a call「致電給某人」。

(B) 題目並未詢問時間，此外，這個回應通常是針對封閉式問題（Yes／No 問句），而題目為開放性問題，兩者互相衝突。

(C) 詢問對方要多少數量，答非所問。

💡 應試者能理解問題的目的，才能選出最適切的答案。

💡 應試者能理解說話者想要表達的意思，有時甚至是隱含的意思。

19. Can understand details in short spoken texts

Can we begin production this week, or should we revise the timeline?

(A) Improving efficiency.
(B) I've seen that performance.
(C) You can start this Thursday.

我們可以在這週開始生產，或是我們應該要修改時程表？

(A) 提高效率。
(B) 我看過那場表演。
(C) 本週四你就可以開始 (生產)。

正解 (C)

重點解說

題目用「... or ...?」詢問對方兩者擇一的情況：要這週開始生產或是要修改時程。選項 (C) 明確說明時間，可以從本週四開始，符合語意，故為正解。production「生產」，revise「修改」，timeline「時程」。

(A) 題目並未詢問效率的改善。improve「改善」，efficiency「效率」。
(B) 題目與表演無關。performance「表演」。

💡 應試者能理解問題及選項的句法，才能選出最適切的答案。

---

20. Can understand details in short spoken texts

Our supervisor booked the tickets for us, right?

(A) I haven't read that book before.
(B) That sounds like it was a long flight.
(C) No, she asked Mary to do it.

我們的主管幫我們訂了票，對嗎？

(A) 我以前沒有讀過那本書。
(B) 這聽起來像是長途飛行。
(C) 不，她叫 Mary 去做的。

正解 (C)

重點解說

題目用附加問句向對方確認主管是否已經幫他們訂票，book 為動詞「預定」。選項 (C) 以 no 開頭，接續說明主管是請 Mary 做這件事，it 代表題目提到的 book the ticket「訂票」，故為正解。supervisor「主管」。

(A) 題目中也有提到 book，但這裡是做名詞使用，與題目無關。
(B) flight「航班」雖看似與題目中的 ticket 有關，但題目並未詢問有關航班的時長。

💡 應試者能理解問題及選項的句法，才能選出最適切的答案。

---

21. Can infer gist, purpose and basic context based on information that is explicitly stated in short spoken texts

Can understand a speaker's purpose or implied meaning in a phrase or sentence

Do you mind if I leave early today?

(A) Has your report been submitted?
(B) Twelve staff members attended.
(C) A 50-dollar discount.

你介意我今天提早離開嗎？

(A) 你的報告提交了嗎？
(B) 有 12 位員工參加。
(C) 50 元的折扣優惠。

正解 (A)

重點解說

「Do you mind if...?」詢問對方是否同意他提早離開，選項 (A) 雖然不是直接回答 Yes／No，而是以問句反問對方「是否已繳交報告」，由此可推斷問話者要先把報告完成才能提早離開，合乎邏輯，故為正解。submit「繳交」。

(B) 題目並未詢問參與人數。attend「參與」。
(C) 題目並未詢問折扣優惠。discount「折扣」。

💡 應試者能理解問題的目的，才能選出最適切的答案。
💡 應試者能理解說話者想要表達的意思，有時甚至是隱含的意思。

22.

Can infer gist, purpose and basic context based on information that is explicitly stated in short spoken texts

Can understand a speaker's purpose or implied meaning in a phrase or sentence

Where are we meeting our clients for lunch?

(A) They had to cancel.
(B) About an account.
(C) Today, at noon.

我們和客戶約在哪裡碰面吃午餐？

(A) 他們必須要取消了。
(B) 關於一個帳戶。
(C) 今天中午。

正解 (A)

重點解說

「Where...?」詢問要與客戶在哪裡碰面吃午餐，選項 (A) 雖然沒有直接回覆地點，但提到某事必須取消，故可推斷 they 指的是客戶，而午餐碰面必須被取消，此為合理回應。had to 為 have to 的過去式。cancel「取消」。
(B) 題目並未詢問 account「帳戶」相關問題。
(C) 題目並未詢問時間。

💡 應試者能理解問題的目的，才能選出最適切的答案。

💡 應試者能理解說話者想要表達的意思，有時甚至是隱含的意思。

23.

Can infer gist, purpose and basic context based on information that is explicitly stated in short spoken texts

Twenty people signed up for the team-building seminar.

(A) The building was renovated.
(B) My favorite sports team.
(C) Great, that's more than last year.

有 20 人報名參加團隊建立研討會。

(A) 這棟大樓翻新了。
(B) 我最喜歡的運動隊伍。
(C) 太棒了，比去年還要多。

正解 (C)

重點解說

直述句敘述「有 20 個人報名參加團隊建立研討會。」選項 (C) 提到參與人數比去年多，明確說明參與狀況，符合語意，故為正解。team-building「團隊建立」，seminar「研討會」。
(A) 雖然選項中也有提到 building，但在此是做名詞，「建築物」的意思，答非所問。renovate「翻新」。
(B) 題目中有提到 team，但選項在回應最喜歡的球隊，答非所問。

💡 應試者能理解題目中說話者所提供的內容及想表達的目的，才能選出最適切的答案。

24.

Can infer gist, purpose and basic context based on information that is explicitly stated in short spoken texts

Can understand a speaker's purpose or implied meaning in a phrase or sentence

Did the cleaning service confirm for next Friday?

(A) The event was a huge success!
(B) I haven't checked my messages yet.
(C) Because it was dirty.

下週五的清潔服務確認了嗎？

(A) 這個活動取得巨大的成功。
(B) 我還沒有查看我的訊息。
(C) 因為這很髒。

正解 (B)

重點解說

通常以助動詞「Did...?」為開頭的問句，要用 Yes／No 回答。選項 (B) 雖然沒有直接回應 Yes／No，但有說明尚未查看訊息，藉此說明還不清楚清潔服務是否已確認下週五的時間，故為正解。confirm「確認」，check「查看」，message「訊息」。
(A) 題目與活動成功與否無關。
(C) dirty「髒的」雖然看似與題目的 cleaning service 有關，但題目並未詢問原因，答非所問。

💡 應試者能理解問題的目的，才能選出最適切的答案。

💡 應試者能理解說話者想要表達的意思，有時甚至是隱含的意思。

25. Can infer gist, purpose and basic context based on information that is explicitly stated in short spoken texts

Can understand a speaker's purpose or implied meaning in a phrase or sentence

How are we marketing our new beverage to young people?

(A) Some pencils and notebooks, please.
(B) Robert's in charge of that product.
(C) Thanks, I'll just have water.

我們該如何向年輕族群行銷我們的新飲料？

(A)（請給我）一些鉛筆和筆記本，謝謝。
(B) Robert 負責該產品。
(C) 謝謝，我只要水就好了。

正解 (B)

重點解說

「How...?」詢問該如何向年輕人行銷新飲料，選項 (B) 雖然沒有直接回答行銷方式，但提到 Robert 負責此產品，推斷出他會負責行銷，符合語意，故為正解。market「行銷」，beverage「飲料」，in charge of「負責」。
(A) pencils 和 notebooks 與題目完全無關。
(C) water 雖看似與題目的 beverage 有關，但整句內容與題目無關，答非所問。

💡 應試者能理解問題的目的，才能選出最適切的答案。
💡 應試者能理解說話者想要表達的意思，有時甚至是隱含的意思。

26. Can infer gist, purpose and basic context based on information that is explicitly stated in short spoken texts

I think we should hire a consultant.

(A) That's not such a bad idea.
(B) Several new employees.
(C) Let's put it on the bottom shelf.

我認為我們應該聘請一位顧問。

(A) 那還真是個不錯的主意。
(B) 一些新的員工。
(C) 讓我們把它放在最下面的架子。

正解 (A)

重點解說

直述句表示說話者認為應該招聘一位顧問的想法，選項 (A) 用「那還真是個不錯的主意。」來回應對方，這句常用來表示同意他人的意見，such「如此、這麼」用來強調肯定這項提議，故為正解。hire「招聘」，consultant「顧問」。
(B) employee「員工」雖與招聘有關，但並未回應到題目，答非所問。
(C) 題目並未討論東西放置的位子。bottom「底部的」，shelf「架子」。

💡 應試者能理解說話者所說的內容及想表達的目的，才能選出最適切的回應。

27. Can infer gist, purpose and basic context based on information that is explicitly stated in short spoken texts

Can understand a speaker's purpose or implied meaning in a phrase or sentence

Where can I get a laptop for our meeting?

(A) The conference room has computers.
(B) Yes, they're doing internships.
(C) We meet once a week.

我可以在哪裡取得我們會議用的筆記型電腦？

(A) 會議室裡有電腦。
(B) 是的，他們正在實習。
(C) 我們每週見一次面。

正解 (A)

重點解說

「Where...?」詢問該到哪裡取得會議用的筆記型電腦，選項 (A) 雖然沒有正面回答，但說明會議室有電腦，由此可推測會議將在會議室舉行，代表不需要借用電腦，符合語意，故為正解。conference room「會議室」。
(B) 問題並未詢問實習相關的問題。internship「實習」。
(C) 題目並未詢問開會頻率。once a week「一週一次」。

💡 應試者能理解問題的目的，才能選出最適切的答案。
💡 應試者能理解說話者想要表達的意思，有時甚至是隱含的意思。

28. ▎Can understand details in short spoken texts

Does the company own or rent its office building?

(A) Have you created an account?

(B) I'm looking for a two-bedroom place.

(C) I believe they're renting.

這棟辦公大樓是公司自有的或是承租的？

(A) 你建立帳戶了嗎？

(B) 我正在尋找一個兩房的住所。

(C) 我認為他們是承租的。

> **正解 (C)**
>
> 重點解說
>
> 通常以助動詞「Does...?」為開頭的問句，要用 Yes／No 回答。題目詢問公司是自有或是承租辦公室大樓，選項 (C) 雖然沒有直接回應 Yes／No，但明確回答「我認為他們是承租的」，為合理回應，故為正解。
> (A) 反問對方有無建立帳戶，答非所問。
> (B) 回答正在尋找兩房的住所，答非所問。look for「尋找」。
>
> 💡 應試者能理解題目及選項中的單字及句法，才能選出最適切的回應。

29. ▎Can infer gist, purpose and basic context based on information that is explicitly stated in short spoken texts

I'm going to pick up the printing order now.

(A) Yes, it was really fun.

(B) Don't forget the receipt.

(C) No, in alphabetical order.

我正要去拿印刷的訂單。

(A) 是的，這真的很有趣。

(B) 不要忘了收據。

(C) 不，要依照字母順序排列。

> **正解 (B)**
>
> 重點解說
>
> 直述句說明「我正要去拿印刷的訂單」，選項 (B) 提到收據，通常付款購買東西後有收據，由此可推知回答者要說話者記得拿收據，為合理回應，故為正解。pick up「拿」，printing「印刷」，order「訂單」，receipt「收據」。
> (A)、(C) 皆以 Yes／No 回應，與題目無關。alphabetical「按字母順序」。
>
> 💡 應試者能理解題目及選項有關訂購相關的內容及說話者的目的，才能選出最適切的答案。

30. ▎Can infer gist, purpose and basic context based on information that is explicitly stated in short spoken texts
▎Can understand a speaker's purpose or implied meaning in a phrase or sentence

When is the new amusement park scheduled to open?

(A) Probably in the city center.

(B) There's an announcement in the newspaper.

(C) Ten cents a copy.

新的遊樂園預計何時開幕？

(A) 大概在市中心。

(B) 報紙上有公告。

(C) 一份 10 分錢。

> **正解 (B)**
>
> 重點解說
>
> 「When...?」詢問新的遊樂園預計何時開幕，選項 (B) 雖未正面回應時間，但提到報紙上有公告，可推測是關於開幕時間的公告，符合語意，故為正解。amusement park「遊樂園」，scheduled「預計」，announcement「公告」。
> (A) 題目並未詢問地點。
> (C) 回答一份 10 分錢，答非所問。
>
> 💡 應試者能理解問題的目的，才能選出最適切的答案。
> 💡 應試者能理解說話者想要表達的意思，有時甚至是隱含的意思。

31.

> Can infer gist, purpose and basic context based on information that is explicitly stated in short spoken texts

> Can understand a speaker's purpose or implied meaning in a phrase or sentence

Does this job candidate have good money-management skills?

(A) I have her résumé right here.
(B) The bank is closed on Sundays.
(C) A very short commute.

這位求職者是否具有良好的理財技能？

(A) 我這裡有她的履歷。
(B) 銀行週日不營業。
(C) 很短的通勤時間。

重點解說

正解 (A)

通常以助動詞「Does...?」為開頭的問句，要用 Yes ／ No 回答。題目詢問求職者是否有良好的理財技能，選項 (A) 雖未直接回應 Yes ／ No，但回覆「我這裡有她的履歷。」隱含意思是對方可自行查看求職者的履歷來得知訊息。job candidate「求職者」，résumé「履歷」。
(B) 選項中的 bank 雖然與題目中的 money-management 有關，但與求職者或技能無關，答非所問。
(C) 題目並未詢問通勤時間。commute「通勤」。

💡 應試者能理解問題的目的，才能選出最適切的答案。

💡 應試者能理解說話者想要表達的意思，有時甚至是隱含的意思。

題目/中文翻譯

Questions 32 through 34 refer to the following conversation.

W: Hi, Jorge. ❶ How's preparation coming along for the new sculpture exhibit?

M: Well, we're a little bit behind actually... ❷the Museum of Plastic Arts is loaning us several sculptures, but ❸ the shipment's been delayed.

W: Oh, no. Is there any way I can help?

M: Well... the rest of the sculptures should be here this afternoon, and this is the list of things that still need to get done.

W: Hmm... how about you finish setting up the final pieces, and ❹ I'll upload photographs of the completed displays to our Web site?

M: That'd be great—thanks!

請參考以下對話內容，回答第 32 至 34 題。

女：嗨，Jorge。新雕塑展的準備工作進展如何？

男：嗯，事實上我們進度有一點落後…造型藝術博物館借給我們許多雕塑品，但是運送延遲了。

女：喔，不。有任何我可以幫忙的地方嗎？

男：嗯…剩下的雕塑品應該在今天下午就會送達，而這是仍要完成事項的清單。

女：嗯…不如你先完成最後作品的布置，而我將已完成的展示照片上傳到我們的網站上？

男：那太好了，謝啦！

---

32. ┃ Can infer gist, purpose and basic context based on information that is explicitly stated in extended spoken texts

Where does the conversation most likely take place?

(A) At a library
(B) At a theater
(C) At a museum
(D) At a restaurant

這段對話最有可能在哪裡發生？

(A) 圖書館
(B) 電影院
(C) 博物館
(D) 餐廳

重點解說

正解 (C)
❶一開始女子詢問男子雕塑展準備的狀況，男子除了回覆進度外，也說明❷另一間博物館出借許多雕塑品。由此可知，對話應是在博物館進行。take place「發生」，sculpture「雕塑」，exhibit「展覽」。
(B) theater「戲院、電影院」。

💡 應試者能聽懂此段對話，並就內容推論對話發生的地點。

33. Can understand details in extended spoken texts

What problem does the man mention?

(A) A brochure contains an error.
(B) A shipment is late.
(C) A guest list has been misplaced.
(D) A computer is not working.

男子提出了什麼問題？

(A) 宣傳手冊裡有一個錯誤。
(B) 運送延遲。
(C) 賓客名單放錯位置。
(D) 電腦出現問題。

重點解說

正解 (B)

❸男子提到運送已經延遲，這對男子來說是個問題。選項 (B) 中的 late 也有 delay「延遲」的意思。shipment「運送」。

(A) 對話中並未提及宣傳手冊。brochure「宣傳手冊」，contain「含有、包括」，error「錯誤」。

(C) 對話中並未提及賓客名單。guest list「賓客名單」，misplace「錯置」。

(D) 對話中並未提及電腦運作狀況。

💡 應試者能理解對話中男子所提到的狀況細節。

34. Can understand details in extended spoken texts

What will the woman most likely do next?

(A) Contact a coordinator
(B) Submit a work order
(C) Upload some images
(D) Purchase some supplies

女子接下來最有可能做什麼事？

(A) 聯繫策展人
(B) 提交一份工作單
(C) 上傳一些圖片
(D) 購買一些補給品

重點解說

正解 (C)

❹女子說「我將已完成的展示照片上傳到我們的網站。」photograph「照片」，選項 (C) 中的 image「影像、畫面」也有類似的意思，故為正解。

(A) contact「聯絡」，coordinator「協調者」。

(B) submit「提交」。

(D) purchase「購買」，supplies「用品」。

💡 應試者能理解對話中女子所說的細節，藉此得知她接下來將會做什麼。

PART 3

Questions 35 through 37 refer to the following conversation.

W: Oh, Jason—❶ the people at table two asked for an order of French fries. They said they forgot to tell you when you took their order.

M: Is that a small or large order of fries?

W: Small.

M: Thanks for letting me know. ❷ I'll go tell the cooks to add it to their order.

W: Great. Oh, by the way, ❸ do you think you could take my shift this Thursday from twelve to five? I forgot I have a dentist appointment.

M: Uh... I have tickets to a baseball game on Thursday.

W: OK, no problem.

請參考以下對話內容，回答第 35 至 37 題。

女：喔，Jason，二號桌的客人點了一份薯條，他們說你在幫他們點餐時，他們忘記告訴你了。

男：是小份或大份的薯條呢？

女：小份的。

男：謝謝你讓我知道，我會去告訴廚師幫他們加點。

女：太好了。喔，順便問一下，你覺得這個週四 12 點到 5 點你可以幫我代班嗎？我忘了我有預約牙醫。

男：呃…我有週四棒球比賽的票。

女：好的，沒問題。

35. Can infer gist, purpose and basic context based on information that is explicitly stated in extended spoken texts

Who most likely are the speakers?

(A) Cleaners
(B) Servers
(C) Nutritionists
(D) Food critics

說話者最有可能是誰？

(A) 清潔人員
(B) 服務生
(C) 營養師
(D) 美食評論家

重點解說

正解 **(B)**

❶一開始女子告知男子二桌的客人要加點薯條，因為他們一開始點餐時忘了告知男子。由此內容推測對話的兩人皆為服務生。order「點餐」，server「服務生」。

💡 應試者能聽懂此段對話，並就內容推論說話者的工作。

36.

Can understand details in extended spoken texts

Why will the man talk to some cooks?

(A) To compliment their work
(B) To ask for some advice
(C) To change an assignment
(D) To update an order

為什麼男子要和廚師說話？

(A) 稱讚他們的工作
(B) 尋求一些建議
(C) 變更任務內容
(D) 更新訂單

重點解說

正解 (D)

❷男子提到「我會去告訴廚師幫他們加點」，it 代表❶提到的薯條。update「更新」。

(A) compliment「讚美」。
(B) ask for「找、尋求」，advice「建議」。
(C) assignment「任務、功課」。

💡 應試者能理解對話中男子所提到的狀況細節。

37.

Can infer gist, purpose and basic context based on information that is explicitly stated in extended spoken texts

Can understand a speaker's purpose or implied meaning in a phrase or sentence

What does the man mean when he says, "I have tickets to a baseball game on Thursday"?

(A) He cannot help the woman.
(B) He has similar interests as the woman.
(C) He wants to invite the woman to an event.
(D) He is concerned that tickets will sell out.

男子說「I have tickets to a baseball game on Thursday」代表什麼意思？

(A) 他沒有辦法幫助女子。
(B) 他和女子有相似的興趣。
(C) 他想邀請女子參加活動。
(D) 他擔心票會賣完。

重點解說

正解 (A)

❸女子詢問男子這週四能否代班，男子接著以「Uh...」猶豫的語氣開頭，並表示「我有週四棒球比賽的票。」代表他那天打算要去看球賽，無法幫女子代班。take one's shift「代某人的班」。

(B) similar「類似的」，interest「興趣」。
(C) invite「邀請」。
(D) concern「擔心」，sell out「賣光、銷售一空」。

💡 應試者能從對話中的資訊推論出大意及說話者的意圖。

💡 即使在回應中，說話者沒有給予正面答覆，應試者仍能從回應中理解其真正想表達的意思。

Questions 38 through 40 refer to the following conversation.

請參考以下對話內容，回答第 38 至 40 題。

W: Carl, ❶ I finished reviewing the finances for our grocery store over the past six months. We're already making a profit! This turned out to be a great location for the new grocery store.

M: That's great news. You know, ❷ I was looking at an appliance catalog, and there's some useful equipment in there. Since we have extra money, why don't we invest in a bigger freezer for our frozen foods section?

W: Good idea. But hmm...are you sure we have enough space for a bigger freezer? ❸ Let me take a look at the floor plan before we make a decision.

女：Carl，我審視了過去六個月我們雜貨店的財務狀況，我們已經開始獲利了！事實證明，這是新雜貨店的絕佳位置。

男：真是個好消息。你知道的，我在看一本電器型錄，裡面有一些有用的設備。既然我們有額外的資金，何不為我們的冷凍食品區投資一個更大的冷凍櫃呢？

女：好主意。但是，嗯…你確定我們有足夠的空間放更大的冷凍櫃嗎？在我們做決定之前，讓我來看一下平面圖。

38. Can understand details in extended spoken texts

What type of business do the speakers own?

(A) A grocery store
(B) A moving company
(C) A construction company
(D) An accounting firm

說話者擁有什麼類型的事業？

(A) 雜貨店
(B) 搬家公司
(C) 建設公司
(D) 會計師事務所

重點解說

正解 (A)
❶ 女子一開始便說明「我審視了我們雜貨店的財務狀況。」由此可知，說話者擁有一間雜貨店。finance「財務狀況」。

💡 應試者能聽懂此段對話以得知說話者所在的產業。

39. | Can understand details in extended spoken texts

What does the man suggest doing?

(A) Extending business hours
(B) Buying new equipment
(C) Hiring more employees
(D) Advertising online

男子建議做什麼？

(A) 延長營業時間
(B) 購買新的設備
(C) 聘請更多員工
(D) 在網路上登廣告

重點解說

正解 (B)

❷ 男子提到「我在看電器型錄，裡面有一些有用的設備。既然有額外的資金，何不為冷凍食物區投資一個更大的冷凍櫃。」由此可知他建議購買新的設備。appliance catalog「電器型錄」，equipment「設備」，invest「投資」，freezer「冷凍櫃」，frozen「冷凍的」。
(A) extend「延長」。
(C) employee「員工」。
(D) advertise「登廣告、宣傳」。

💡 應試者能理解對話中男子所提到的狀況細節。

40. | Can understand details in extended spoken texts

What does the woman say she will do?

(A) Review a budget
(B) Consult an expert
(C) Print an inventory list
(D) Check a floor plan

女子說她將會做什麼？

(A) 審查預算
(B) 諮詢專家
(C) 列印庫存清單
(D) 檢查平面圖

重點解說

正解 (D)

❸ 女子說「在我們做決定前，讓我看一下平面圖。」選項 (D) 中的 check 與女子說的 take a look 有相似的意思，故為正解。floor plan「平面圖」。
(A) budget「預算」。
(B) consult「諮詢」，expert「專家」。
(C) inventory list「庫存清單」。

💡 應試者能理解對話中女子所說的細節，藉此得知她接下來將會做什麼。

Questions 41 through 43 refer to the following conversation.

M: Lopez and Sons. How can I help you?

W: Hello, I'm calling about my car. My last name's Delgado.

M: Yes, Ms. Delgado. ❶ We've found a problem with your car battery. Would you like us to install a new one?

W: How much will that be?

M: ❷ A new battery costs 100 dollars to install.

W: OK, that's fine. Hmm, ❸ I was also planning to get my tires replaced soon. How much is that?

M: ❹ That depends on the kind of tires you want. We have a brochure listing the different options. ❺ I can give you one when you come in to pick up your car.

請參考以下對話內容，回答第 41 至 43 題。

男：Lopez and Sons，有什麼我可以協助您的嗎？

女：你好，我打電話來詢問我的車。我姓 Delgado。

男：是的，Delgado 小姐。我們發現您的汽車電池有問題，您想讓我們安裝一個新的嗎？

女：那要多少錢呢？

男：安裝新的電池需要 100 元。

女：好的，沒問題。嗯，我近期也計畫要更換我的輪胎。那要多少錢呢？

男：看您想要什麼種類的輪胎。我們有一本手冊列出不同的規格，當您過來牽車時，我可以給您一本。

41.

Can infer gist, purpose and basic context based on information that is explicitly stated in extended spoken texts

Where does the man most likely work?

(A) At a car repair shop
(B) At a manufacturing plant
(C) At a taxi service
(D) At a law office

男子最有可能在哪裡工作？

(A) 修車廠
(B) 製造工廠
(C) 計程車服務處
(D) 律師事務所

重點解說

正解 (A)

❶男子提到「我們發現您的汽車電池有問題。」並接著詢問女子是否要幫她安裝一個新的。在❸與❹兩個人也有在討論更換輪胎。由此可推知，男子是在修車廠工作。battery「電池」，install「安裝」，repair「修理」。
(C) taxi「計程車」。雖看似與汽車電池可能有關，但後續對話並未提及計程車相關訊息。

💡 應試者能理解生活情境的相關單字，以推論出說話者的工作地點。

42. Can understand details in extended spoken texts

What does the woman ask the man about?

(A) A project deadline
(B) A logo design
(C) The cost of some services
(D) The quality of some materials

女子詢問男子什麼事情？

(A) 專案的截止日期
(B) 商標的設計
(C) 某些服務的費用
(D) 某些材料的品質

重點解說

正解 (C)
由❷男子提到安裝新的電池要 100 元，可以得知是回答女子安裝的費用。❸女子後續又詢問更換輪胎的費用，這些都屬於修車廠的服務。
(A) 女子並未詢問截止日期。deadline「截止日期」。
(B) logo「商標」。
(D) quality「品質」，material「材料」。

💡 應試者能理解對話中女子所提及的細節。

43. Can understand details in extended spoken texts

What does the man say he will give to the woman?

(A) A brochure
(B) A discount
(C) Free delivery
(D) Sample products

男子說他將會給女子什麼東西？

(A) 手冊
(B) 折扣
(C) 免費運送
(D) 樣品

重點解說

正解 (A)
❹男子說，看您想要哪種輪胎，我們手冊中有列出不同的規格，並於❺提到，當女子過來牽車時，可以給她一本，句中提到的 one 指的是❹提到的 brochure，故選項 (A) 為正解。

💡 應試者能理解對話中男子所說的細節。

Questions 44 through 46 refer to the following conversation.

M: Hi, Leticia. I wanted to update you about the discussion I had yesterday with our legal team about the company merger.

W: OK. ❶ I heard we're still on track to complete the merger by the end of the year.

M: Right. Well, there's a problem. ❷ We're having trouble agreeing on what the logo for the new company should be when we merge. They rejected the designs that you and your marketing team proposed.

W: Hmm. OK. ❸ I'll schedule a meeting with my team so we can come up with something else. Let me set that up right now.

請參考以下對話內容，回答第 44 至 46 題。

男：嗨，Leticia。我想跟妳更新一下我昨天與我們的法務團隊就公司合併進行的討論。

女：好的，我聽說我們仍能順利在年底前完成合併。

男：是的，但是有一個問題。對於合併後新公司的 Logo 我們無法達成共識，他們拒絕了妳和妳的行銷團隊提出的設計。

女：嗯，好的。我將會和我的團隊安排一個會議以提出其他可能。我現在就來安排。

44. | Can understand details in extended spoken texts

What will take place this year?

(A) A corporate merger
(B) A software update
(C) A research study
(D) An office relocation

今年將會發生什麼事？

(A) 公司合併
(B) 軟體更新
(C) 研究調查
(D) 辦公室搬遷

重點解說

正解 (A)

❶女子提及「我聽說我們仍能順利在年底前完成合併。」由此可知，今年將進行公司合併。on track「進展順利」，complete「完成」，take place「發生」，corporate「公司的」，merger「合併」。
(B) software「軟體」。
(D) relocation「搬遷、更換地點」。

💡 應試者能聽懂此段對話以得知是發生何種事件。

45. | Can understand details in extended spoken texts

What problem does the man mention? | 男子提到什麼問題？

(A) Some paperwork has been lost. | (A) 有些文件遺失了。
(B) Some equipment is broken. | (B) 有些設備損壞了。
(C) Some funding was not approved. | (C) 有些資金未獲批准。
(D) Some designs were rejected. | **(D) 有些設計被拒絕了。**

正解 (D)

❷男子提到雙方在新公司的商標上有不同意見，對方駁回團隊的設計。have trouble + Ving「有困難做某事」，reject「駁回」，propose「提出」。
(A) 對話並未提及文件遺失，paperwork「文件、資料」。
(B) equipment「設備」，broken「損壞的」。
(C) funding「資金」，approve「核可」。

💡 應試者能理解對話中男子所提到的狀況細節。

---

46. | Can understand details in extended spoken texts

What will the woman do next? | 女子接下來將會做什麼？

(A) Revise a budget | (A) 修改預算
(B) Schedule a meeting | **(B) 安排一個會議**
(C) Find some contact information | (C) 找一些聯絡資訊
(D) Hire a consultant | (D) 聘請顧問

正解 (B)

❸女子說「我將會和我的團隊安排一個會議以提出其他可能。」come up with sth「想出、提出（主意或計畫）」。
(A) revise「修改」，budget「預算」。
(C) contact「聯絡」。
(D) consultant「顧問」。

💡 應試者能理解對話中女子所說的細節，藉此得知她接下來將會做什麼。

Questions 47 through 49 refer to the following conversation with three speakers.

請參考以下三人對話內容，回答第 47 至 49 題。

M1 : Kentaro, ❶ another television unit just failed the quality-control check right off the assembly line.

M2 : What was wrong with it? Was it the screen?

M1 : No, worse. ❷ It wouldn't turn on at all. That's the third one today. There seems to be a problem with the electrical wiring.

M2 : Who's the supervisor on duty today?

M1 : Ms. Takano. There she is. Ms. Takano?

W : Is everything all right?

M1 : We've had several televisions fail quality control.

W : Thank you for telling me. ❸ I'll call an engineer.

男1：Kentaro，又一台剛在生產線組裝好的電視機沒通過品管檢驗。

男2：發生什麼問題？是螢幕嗎？

男1：不，更糟糕，它根本無法開機了。這是今天的第三起事件，看起來似乎是電子線路有問題。

男2：今天值班的主管是誰？

男1：Takano小姐。她在那邊。是Takano小姐嗎？

女 ：一切都還好嗎？

男1：有幾台電視機沒有通過品管。

女 ：謝謝你告訴我，我會打電話給工程師。

---

47. | Can infer gist, purpose and basic context based on information that is explicitly stated in extended spoken texts

Where most likely are the speakers?

這些說話者最有可能在什麼地方？

(A) At a storage facility

(B) At an electronics factory

(C) At a film studio

(D) At a technology exhibition

(A) 倉儲

(B) 電子工廠

(C) 電影攝影棚

(D) 科技展

重點解說

正解 **(B)**

❶一開始男子說明有另一組電視才剛組裝好，卻沒通過品管測試，由此可知，說話者們應是在電子工廠談話。fail「失敗、未能做到」，quality-control check「品管檢驗」，assembly line「生產線」。

(A) storage「儲藏」，facility「場所、機構」。

(C) film「影片」，studio「攝影棚、錄音室」。

(D) exhibition「展覽」。

💡 應試者能聽懂此段對話，並就內容推論說話者所在場所。

48. Can infer gist, purpose and basic context based on information that is explicitly stated in extended spoken texts

What problem are the men discussing?

(A) Some products are defective.
(B) A container is not large enough.
(C) There are not enough workers.
(D) An order was canceled.

男子們在討論什麼問題？

(A) 有些產品有瑕疵。
(B) 貨櫃尺寸不夠大。
(C) 工人不足。
(D) 一張訂單被取消。

重點解說

正解 (A)

❷男子提到已是第三組才組裝好卻無法開機的電視，他還提到電視內部電子線路的潛在問題，故可推斷出他們在討論一些有缺陷的產品，故選項 (A) 為正解。defective「有缺陷的」。
(B) container「容器、貨櫃」。

💡 應試者能理解職場領域相關單字，以得知對話中男子們所討論的狀況。

49. Can understand details in extended spoken texts

What does the woman say she will do?

(A) Offer a discount
(B) Renegotiate a contract
(C) Inspect a shipment
(D) Notify an engineer

女子說她將會做什麼事？

(A) 提供折扣
(B) 重新協商合約
(C) 檢查貨物
(D) 通知工程師

重點解說

正解 (D)

❸女子說「我會打電話給工程師。」選項 (D) 通知工程師，notify「通知」與對話中女子說的 call「致電」意思類似。
(B) renegotiate「重新協商」。
(C) inspect「檢查」，shipment「運輸的貨物」。

💡 應試者能理解對話中女子所說的細節，藉此得知她接下來將會做什麼。

Questions 50 through 52 refer to the following conversation.

請參考以下對話內容，回答第 50 至 52 題。

W: ❶ Welcome to Jackson Pharmacy. Can I help you?

女：歡迎來到 Jackson 藥局。有什麼我可以幫你嗎？

M: Hi. I'm here to pick up some allergy medication. My doctor recommended that I take the kind called Valgone.

男：你好，我來這裡買一些過敏藥。我的醫生建議我服用一種叫 Valgone 的藥。

W: Sure, let me check if we have any. ❷ Oh... unfortunately we don't have any available at the moment. That's a popular medication.

女：沒問題，讓我看一下我們有沒有這種藥。喔…很不湊巧，我們目前沒有任何庫存，這是一款熱門的藥。

M: I guess I should've called first.

男：我想我應該要先打電話。

W: ❸ We should get that medication in soon, if you'd like to come back in a couple of days. Why don't you write your name here, and we'll put some aside for you.

女：如果你想要過幾天再回來，我們應該可以很快進到這種藥。你何不把你的名字寫在這裡，我們會為你保留。

M: OK, thanks. ❹ I'll come back later in the week.

男：好，謝謝。我這週會再過來。

50. | Can understand details in extended spoken texts

Where are the speakers?

(A) At a pharmacy
(B) At a clothing store
(C) At a dental clinic
(D) At a fitness center

說話者在哪裡？

(A) 藥局
(B) 服飾店
(C) 牙醫診所
(D) 健身中心

重點解說

正解 (A)

❶一開始女子便以藥局名稱開頭招呼，由此可知說話者所在位置。pharmacy「藥局」。

(B) clothing「衣服、服飾」。

(C) dental「牙齒的」，clinic「診所」。

💡 應試者能聽懂此段對話以得知對話發生的地點。

51. | Can understand details in extended spoken texts |

What does the woman explain to the man?

(A) He has missed an appointment.
(B) A price has changed.
(C) A business is closing soon.
(D) An item is not available.

女子向男子解釋什麼？

(A) 他已經錯過預約。
(B) 價格已經改變。
(C) 公司快結束營業。
(D) 商品沒有貨。

重點解說

正解 (D)

❷ 女子說明「很不湊巧，我們目前沒有任何庫存。」選項 (D) item「品項」指的是對話中的藥，故為正解。unfortunately「可惜地」，available「可用的、可得的」，at the moment「此刻」。
(A) appointment「約會、預約」。
(B) 對話中並未提到價格有改變。
(C) business 在此作為「公司」，對話中並未提到有公司要結束營業。

💡 應試者能理解對話中女子所提到的狀況細節。

---

52. | Can understand details in extended spoken texts |

What does the man say he will do?

(A) Complete a customer survey
(B) Return another day
(C) Look up some data
(D) Pay with a credit card

男子說他將會做什麼？

(A) 完成一份顧客調查
(B) 改天再過來
(C) 查找一些資料
(D) 用信用卡付款

重點解說

正解 (B)

聽完女子說明❸男子所需的藥物很快會到貨，若他願意再過來一趟，他們可以幫他先保留，男子回答❹「我這週會再過來。」return「返回、重回」。
(A) complete「完成」，customer survey「顧客調查」。
(C) look up「查找」，data「數據、資料」。
(D) 對話中並未提及男子要用何種方式付款。

💡 應試者能理解對話中男子所說的細節，藉此得知他接下來將會做什麼。

Questions 53 through 55 refer to the following conversation.

W: ❶ Fly Right Airlines, how can I help you?

M: Hi, I'm calling about a flight I'm taking to Madrid tomorrow. I have a question about luggage. I know that I can check one bag for free, but I'm not sure what the weight limit is.

W: ❷ The weight limit per bag is 23 kilograms.

M: Oh, well... my bag weighs 30 kilograms.

W: Then there will be a charge. I could process that payment for you now if you'd like.

M: Sure, ❸ but I'm in a bit of a hurry. My phone doesn't have much battery power left, and I'm worried that it'll shut down soon.

請參考以下對話內容,回答第 53 至 55 題。

女:Fly Right 航空,有什麼我可以協助您的嗎?

男:妳好,我打電話過來是為了明天我要飛往馬德里的航班。我有一個關於行李的問題,我知道我可以免費託運一件行李,但是我不確定重量限制是多少。

女:每件行李的重量限制是 23 公斤。

男:喔,好吧…我的包包 30 公斤重。

女:那麼將會收取費用。如果您願意,我現在可以為您處理這筆款項。

男:當然可以,但是我有一點趕時間。我的手機沒有多少電量了,我擔心它很快就會關機。

53. ⎰ Can infer gist, purpose and basic context based on information that is explicitly stated in extended spoken texts

What type of business does the woman work for?

(A) A telephone company

(B) An airline company

(C) An accounting firm

(D) A department store

女子在什麼類型的公司工作?

(A) 電話公司

(B) 航空公司

(C) 會計師事務所

(D) 百貨公司

重點解說

正解 (B)

❶女子以航空公司名稱做開頭招呼語,由此可知,女子是在航空公司上班。airline「航空公司」。

💡 應試者能理解生活情境的相關單字,以推論出說話者的工作地點。

54. Can infer gist, purpose and basic context based on information that is explicitly stated in extended spoken texts

Can understand a speaker's purpose or implied meaning in a phrase or sentence

What does the man imply when he says, "my bag weighs 30 kilograms"?

(A) He plans to buy a different bag.
(B) He needs help carrying his bag.
(C) His bag does not have any extra space.
(D) His bag does not meet the requirements.

男子說「my bag weighs 30 kilograms」，暗示了什麼？

(A) 他計畫購買一個不同的包包。
(B) 他需要人幫忙提他的包包。
(C) 他的包包沒有額外的空間。
(D) 他的包包不符合規定。

> 重點解說
>
> 正解 (D)
>
> ❷ 因女子說明每個行李的重量限制為 23 公斤，而男子的行李為 30 公斤，由此可推斷他的行李並沒有符合航空公司的規定，故選項 (D) 為正解。weight「重量」，limit「限制」，kilogram「公斤」，weigh「稱重」，requirement「規定」。
> (A) plan to＋V「計畫做某事」。
> (B) carry「提、拿」。
> (C) extra「額外的」。
>
> 💡 應試者能從對話中的資訊推論出大意及說話者的意圖。
>
> 💡 應試者能理解說話者真正想要表達的意思。

55. Can understand details in extended spoken texts

Why is the man in a hurry?

(A) His flight is about to depart.
(B) His presentation is starting soon.
(C) His phone battery is low.
(D) His taxi is waiting.

為什麼男子很緊急？

(A) 他的航班即將起飛。
(B) 他的演講即將開始。
(C) 他的手機電量不足。
(D) 他的計程車正在等他。

> 重點解說
>
> 正解 (C)
>
> ❸ 男子解釋「我的手機沒有多少電量了，我擔心它很快就會關機。」選項 (C) 以換句話說明相同的狀況「他的手機電量不足。」in a hurry「趕時間」，battery「電池」，shut down「關閉」。
> (A) depart「起飛」。
> (B) presentation「演講」。
> (D) 男子並未提及有計程車在等他。
>
> 💡 應試者能理解對話中男子所說的狀況，藉此推知他趕時間的原因。

Questions 56 through 58 refer to the following conversation.

W: Hi, Anton. My name's Maria and I'll be your manager here at LW Energy Solutions. ❶ Were you able to get your security badge?

M: Glad to be here! And ❷ yes, the camera was acting up a bit, but the personnel office was able to print out the badge all right.

W: OK, great. You'll need that to get into the buildings on-site. So, ❸ let's head on over to the employee cafeteria now, where we can have a light lunch.

M: Sounds good. Um, I noticed that there's a lot of construction going on...

W: Oh, yes! ❹ We're installing solar panels on some of our other buildings here.

請參考以下對話內容，回答第 56 至 58 題。

女：你好，Anton，我的名字是 Maria，而我將會是你在 LW Energy Solutions 的經理。你拿到你的安全識別證了嗎？

男：很高興來到這裡！有的，雖然相機有些小狀況，但人事部門有順利印出識別證。

女：太好了，你會需要它才能進入大樓裡。那麼，我們現在前往員工餐廳吧，在那裡我們可以吃一頓簡餐。

男：聽起來不錯。嗯，我注意到這裡有許多工程正在進行…

女：喔，是的！我們正在一些大樓上安裝太陽能面板。

---

56. | Can understand details in extended spoken texts

What does the man confirm that he has received?

(A) A copy of a contract
(B) An employee manual
(C) A security badge
(D) Some log-in information

男士確認他拿到了什麼？

(A) 一份合約副本
(B) 一本員工手冊
(C) 一個安全識別證
(D) 一些登入的訊息

重點解說

正解 (C)
❶女子在自我介紹後，便詢問男子是否有拿到安全識別證，❷男子回覆「有的，雖然相機有些小狀況，但人事部門後來有順利印出識別證。」security badge「安全識別證」，act up「故障」，personnel office「人事部門」，print out「印出」，confirm「確認」，receive「得到、收到」。
(A) contract「合約」。
(B) employee「員工」，manual「手冊」。
(D) 男子並未提及登入相關問題。

💡 應試者能聽懂此段對話以理解男子所說的狀況。

57. Can understand details in extended spoken texts

Where are the speakers going next?

(A) To an airport
(B) To a cafeteria
(C) To a training workshop
(D) To a client meeting

說話者接下來要去哪裡？

(A) 機場
(B) 自助餐廳
(C) 培訓工作坊
(D) 與客戶開會

重點解說

正解 (B)

❸女子說「我們現在前往員工餐廳吧，在那裡我們可以享用簡餐。」由此可推知說話者將要前往的地點。head on over to「前往」，cafeteria「自助餐廳」。
(C) workshop「工作坊」。
(D) client「客戶」。

💡 應試者能理解對話中說話者所提到的狀況細節。

58. Can understand details in extended spoken texts

What does the woman say is currently happening at the company?

(A) A computer system is being upgraded.
(B) A parking area is being repaired.
(C) Some policies are being revised.
(D) Some solar panels are being installed.

女子說目前公司正在進行什麼事？

(A) 正在升級電腦系統。
(B) 正在維修停車區域。
(C) 正在修訂一些政策。
(D) 正在安裝一些太陽能面板。

重點解說

正解 (D)

❹女子說「我們正在一些大樓上安裝太陽能板。」選項 (D) 以被動語法（be 動詞＋過去分詞）說明此件事。install「安裝」，solar panel「太陽能板」，currently「目前」。
(A) upgrade「升級」。
(B) repair「修理」。
(C) policy「政策」，revise「修改」。

💡 應試者能理解對話中女子所說的細節，藉此得知公司目前發生的狀況。

PART 3

Questions 59 through 61 refer to the following conversation with three speakers.

M1: Good morning, everyone. ❶ I've scheduled this conference call to discuss the advertising campaign we're developing for Denson Hotels— more specifically, the television commercial. Holly will be sharing some preliminary ideas for that. And Carter is joining us by video call from our Tokyo office. Carter, are you there?

M2: Hello. Yes, I'm here.

M1: Great. Holly, you can begin.

W : OK, so I've been working on developing ideas for the commercial—you know, the concept, the setting, and—

M2: Hey guys, this is Carter again. Sorry to interrupt, but the audio suddenly went quiet. Were you saying something?

M1: Uh-oh. ❷ My laptop's microphone must be malfunctioning again.

W : ❸ Let's switch to my laptop. It works well for video calls.

請參考以下三人對話內容，回答第 59 至 61 題。

男 1：大家早安，我安排了這場電話會議來討論 我們正在為 Denson 飯店所規畫的廣告 行銷活動—更準確地說，就是電視廣告。 Holly 將會分享一些初步的想法，而 Carter 正從我們的東京辦公室透過視訊電話參與 我們的會議。Carter，你在嗎？

男 2：哈囉。是的，我在這裡。

男 1：很好。Holly，妳可以開始了。

女 ：好的，我一直在為廣告構思創意—你知道 的，就是概念、設定、以及…

男 2：嗨各位，又是我，Carter。抱歉打斷一下， 但聲音突然沒了。你們剛剛在說什麼嗎？

男 1：呃…喔，我的筆記型電腦的麥克風一定又 故障了。

女 ：換到我的筆記型電腦吧！它在視訊通話下 運作良好。

---

59. Can infer gist, purpose and basic context based on information that is explicitly stated in extended spoken texts

What field do the speakers most likely work in?

(A) Engineering
(B) Accounting
(C) Education
(D) Advertising

說話者最有可能在什麼領域工作？

(A) 工程
(B) 會計
(C) 教育
(D) 廣告

重點解說

正解 (D)

❶男子開頭說，此次安排電話會議是要討論我們為 Denson 飯店所規畫的行銷活動，特別是電視廣告的部分。由 此可知，這群說話者是在行銷產業工作。conference call「電話會議」，campaign「行銷活動」，commercial「廣 告」，field「領域」。

💡 應試者能理解職場情境中常見的部門與功能的相關單字，以推論出說話者的工作。

60. Can understand details in extended spoken texts

What problem is mentioned?

(A) A power cord is missing.
(B) A microphone is not functioning properly.
(C) A screen is not displaying an image.
(D) A battery is not charging.

什麼問題被提出？

(A) 電源線不見了。
(B) 麥克風無法正常運作。
(C) 螢幕無法顯示畫面。
(D) 電池沒有在充電。

重點解說

正解 (B)
❷男子提到「我的筆記型電腦的麥克風一定又故障了。」malfunction「故障」，選項 (B) 說明同樣狀況「麥克風無法正常運作」，故為正解。function「運作」，properly「正常地」。
(A) power cord「電源線」。
(C) display「顯示、播放」。
(D) charge「充電」。

💡 應試者能從對話中理解男子所提到的狀況細節。

61. Can understand details in extended spoken texts

What does the woman suggest doing?

(A) Using a different computer
(B) Moving to another room
(C) Postponing a demonstration
(D) Contacting technical support

女子建議做什麼事情？

(A) 使用另一台電腦
(B) 移動到另一個房間
(C) 延後示範
(D) 聯絡技術支援

重點解說

正解 (A)
❸女子說「換到我的筆記型電腦吧！它在視訊通話下運作良好。」let's「讓我們…」用來表達提議或邀請，switch「替換」，suggest「建議」。
(B) 女子並未提及要更換會議室。
(C) postpone「延遲、延期」，demonstration「示範、展示」。
(D) technical「技術的」。

💡 應試者能理解對話中女子所說的細節，藉此得知她建議要做什麼。

題目 / 中文翻譯

Questions 62 through 64 refer to the following conversation and Web site.

請參考以下對話內容及網站，回答第62至64題。

M: ❶ Bella's Cakes. May I help you?

W: I'd like to order a large chocolate cake.

M: Certainly. Would you like anything special on the cake?

W: Well, it's for an office event. We're a publishing house and we're celebrating the release of a new book. ❷ It's important that the cake is book themed. Can you decorate it to look like a book?

M: Sure, we can do that.

W: Great. ❸ So can I pick it up at six tomorrow evening?

M: ❹ We're only open until five. But, I can take your order, and then you can pick it up from one of our other locations. They're listed on our Web site.

男：Bella's Cake，有什麼我可以效勞的嗎？

女：我想要訂一個大的巧克力蛋糕。

男：沒問題。蛋糕上您想要有任何特別的東西嗎？

女：嗯，這個蛋糕是為了辦公室的活動。我們是一間出版社，我們正在慶祝新書的發行。重要的是蛋糕要以書為主題，你能將它裝飾得像一本書嗎？

男：沒問題，我們可以做到。

女：太棒了，那我可以明天傍晚六點拿蛋糕嗎？

男：我們店只營業到五點。但是，我可以接受您的訂單，你能在我們其他分店之一取貨。店面位置列在我們的網站上。

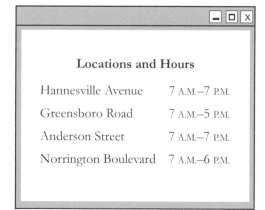

Locations and Hours	
Hannesville Avenue	7 A.M.–7 P.M.
Greensboro Road	7 A.M.–5 P.M.
Anderson Street	7 A.M.–7 P.M.
Norrington Boulevard	7 A.M.–6 P.M.

位置和營業時間	
Hannesville 大街	7 A.M. — 7 P.M.
Greensboro 路	7 A.M. — 5 P.M.
Anderson 街	7 A.M. — 7 P.M.
Norrington 大道	7 A.M. — 6 P.M.

62. Can infer gist, purpose and basic context based on information that is explicitly stated in extended spoken texts

Where does the man work?

(A) At a furniture store
(B) At a painting company
(C) At a bakery
(D) At a gym

男子在哪裡工作？

(A) 家具店
(B) 油漆公司
(C) 麵包店
(D) 健身房

重點解說

正解 **(C)**
由❶男子開頭說 Bella's Cakes，可以推測出男子工作的場所為麵包店。
(A) furniture「家具」。
(B) paint「油漆、顏料」。
💡 應試者能理解常見領域的相關單字，以推論出男子的工作地點。

題目／中文翻譯

63. `Can understand details in extended spoken texts`

What does the woman say is important?

(A) A healthy option
(B) A low price
(C) A fast delivery
(D) A specific decoration

女子說什麼事情很重要？

(A) 健康的選項
(B) 低價
(C) 快速出貨
(D) 特定的裝飾

重點解說

正解 (D)
由❷女子說「蛋糕以書為主題是很重要的，你能將它裝飾得像一本書嗎？」可得知，女子希望蛋糕呈現特定的裝飾，故選項 (D) 為正解。theme「主題」，decorate「裝飾」，specific「特定的」，decoration「裝飾」。
(A) healthy「健康的」，option「選項」。
(B) low「低、小、少的」，price「價格」。
(C) delivery「運送」。

💡 應試者能從對話中理解女子所提到的狀況細節。

64. `Can understand details in extended spoken texts`

Look at the graphic. Which location did the woman call?

(A) Hannesville Avenue
(B) Greensboro Road
(C) Anderson Street
(D) Norrington Boulevard

請看圖。女子致電到哪個店面位置？

(A) Hannesville 大街
(B) Greensboro 路
(C) Anderson 街
(D) Norrington 大道

重點解說

正解 (B)
由❸女子本來詢問「我可以明天傍晚六點拿蛋糕嗎？」❹男子回覆「我們店只營業到五點。」再對照圖表，只有 Greensboro 路上的店面營業到五點，故可得知女子致電的店家位置。pick...up「提取」。
(A) avenue「大街」。
(C) street「（較小的）街道」。
(D) boulevard「大道」。

💡 應試者能理解對話中的細節並對照圖表，藉此得知女子致電的店面位置。

題 目 / 中 文 翻 譯

Questions 65 through 67 refer to the following conversation and coupon.

W: Hi, George. We're all set to open our sporting goods store next week. ❶ As we discussed, we'll be offering special discounts on our opening day.

M: Here, I put together a flyer of coupons that we can give away at the store entrance.

W: Nice. I think the savings on running shoes will get customers into the store, but I've been thinking... ❷ I'm concerned about the discount on camping equipment. We probably won't make money on those sales.

M: I agree. ❸ We should lower the discount by half that amount. ❹ I can make the change and print out a copy.

W: Good. ❺ Then I'll drop it off at the printers first thing tomorrow.

請參考以下對話內容及折價券，回答第 65 至 67 題。

女：嗨，George。下週運動用品店開幕我們都準備好了。如我們先前討論的，我們將在開幕日提供優惠折扣。

男：嘿，我整理了一張折價券的傳單，我們可以在商店入口處發放。

女：很好，我認為跑步鞋省下的錢將會吸引客人進來店裡，但是我一直在思考…我有些擔心露營用品的折扣，我們可能無法在這些促銷上獲利。

男：我同意，我們應該把折扣減半。我可以修改後印一份出來。

女：很好，那麼我明天一早就將它拿去影印店。

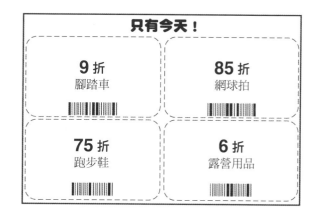

65. `Can infer gist, purpose and basic context based on information that is explicitly stated in extended spoken texts`

What is the occasion for the special sale?

(A) A store anniversary
(B) A public holiday
(C) A grand opening
(D) A customer contest

這場特賣的原因是什麼？

(A) 店家週年慶
(B) 國定假日
(C) 盛大的開幕
(D) 客戶競賽

重點解說

正解 **(C)**
❶ 男子開頭說「如我們先前討論的，我們將在開幕日提供優惠折扣。」選項 (C) grand opening「盛大開幕」也是敘述開幕的說法，故為正解。occasion「原因、時機」。
(A) anniversary「週年紀念日」，對話中商店才剛開幕。
(B) 對話中並未提及國定假日。
(D) contest「比賽、競賽」，對話中並未提及任何比賽。

💡 應試者能理解常見生活情境的相關單字，以推論對話所討論的場合。

66. Can understand details in extended spoken texts

Look at the graphic. Which discount will be changed?

(A) 10%
(B) 15%
(C) 25%
(D) 40%

請看圖。哪一項折扣將會被修改？

(A) 9 折
(B) 85 折
(C) 75 折
(D) 6 折

重點解說

正解 (D)

❷女子先提到「我有些擔心露營用品的折扣。」接著❸男子提出「我們應該把折扣減半。」由此可知說話者討論應該調整露營用品的折扣，看圖可知露營用品原先的折扣為 6 折。concern「擔心」，camping equipment「露營用品」。

💡 應試者能從對話中不同段落理解討論的狀況細節。

67. Can understand details in extended spoken texts

What does the woman say she will do tomorrow?

(A) Receive a shipment
(B) Contact a caterer
(C) Go to a printshop
(D) Organize a display

女子說她明天將會做什麼事？

(A) 收貨
(B) 聯絡外燴業者
(C) 去影印店
(D) 規畫展示品

重點解說

正解 (C)

❺女子說「我明天一早就將它拿去影印店。」句中 it 為❹男子提到「我可以修改後印一份出來」的文件。drop off 是將某物送或拿去某個地點。printer 有「印表機」的意思，也可解釋為「印刷業者、影印店」，而介系詞 at 後方通常可接地點或時間，由此推論 printer 在此是「影印店」，故選項 (C) 為正解。

(A) receive「接收」，shipment「貨運」。

(B) caterer「外燴業者」。

(D) organize「組織、籌畫」，display「展示、陳列」。

💡 應試者能理解對話中女子所說的細節，藉此得知她接下來要做什麼。

Questions 68 through 70 refer to the following conversation and floor plan.

請參考以下對話內容及平面圖，回答第 68 至 70 題。

M: Hello, Tara. ❶ This is Sam Watson, the apartment building manager. Your rental agreement expires July first, and I was wondering if you're planning to renew it.

W: Hi, Sam. To be honest, I haven't decided yet. I like the apartment building and amenities, but I don't like the location of my apartment.

M: Oh, what's the problem?

W: Well, ❷ I have the corner unit across from the stairs. I can hear people talking when they're on the stairs.

M: I understand. Well, there's another apartment available on that same floor that I think you'd like. ❸ It's also a corner unit, but it's the one farthest away from the stairs.

W: That sounds good. Could I see it?

男：Tara，您好。我是公寓大廈經理Sam Watson。您的租約在七月一日到期，所以我想知道您是否打算續約。

女：嗨，Sam。老實說，我還沒有決定。我喜歡這棟公寓大廈和設施，但是我不喜歡我公寓的位置。

男：喔，有什麼問題嗎？

女：是這樣的，我的房間是一間邊間，就在樓梯的對面。每當有人在樓梯上時，我都能聽見他們在說話。

男：我明白了。那麼，在同一層樓有另一間空的公寓，我想您會喜歡的。這間房也是邊間，但它是離樓梯最遠的一間。

女：聽起來不錯，我可以看看嗎？

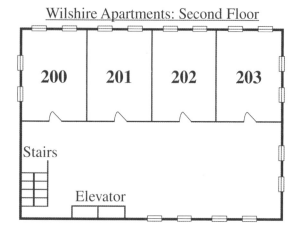

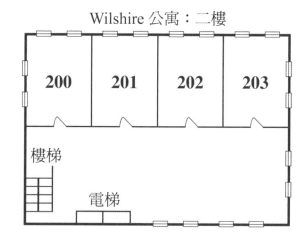

68. Can understand details in extended spoken texts

Who is the man?

(A) A building manager
(B) A delivery driver
(C) A repair person
(D) An interior decorator

男子是何人？

(A) 大樓經理
(B) 送貨司機
(C) 維修人員
(D) 室內設計師

重點解說

正解 **(A)**
❶男子開頭說「我是公寓大廈經理 Sam Watson。」由此可知男子的職業。
(B) delivery「運送」。
(C) repair「維修」。
(D) interior「室內的」，decorator「裝潢設計師」。
💡 應試者能理解對話中男子所說的細節，藉此得知男子的職業。

69. Can understand details in extended spoken texts

What does the woman complain about?

(A) The high cost of a service
(B) The noise outside her apartment
(C) The length of a renovation project
(D) The limited access to parking

女子抱怨什麼事情？

(A) 高昂的服務費
(B) 在她公寓外的噪音
(C) 裝修項目的工期
(D) 停車使用權受限

重點解說

正解 (B)

❷女子提到「我的房間是一間邊間，就在樓梯的對面。每當有人在樓梯上時，我都能聽見他們在說話。」由此可知，女子暗指因為她的房間就在樓梯對面，只要有人在樓梯上談話她都能聽到。選項 (B) noise「噪音」指的是有人在樓梯上說話的聲音，故為正解。corner unit「邊間」，across from「在⋯的對面」，stairs「樓梯」，complain「抱怨」。

(A) cost「費用、成本」。
(C) length「長度」，renovation「裝修」。
(D) access「使用權、進入」。

💡 應試者能從對話中理解女子所提到的狀況細節。

70. Can understand details in extended spoken texts

Look at the graphic. Which apartment does the man mention?

(A) Apartment 200
(B) Apartment 201
(C) Apartment 202
(D) Apartment 203

請看圖。男子提到的公寓是哪一間？

(A) 公寓 200
(B) 公寓 201
(C) 公寓 202
(D) 公寓 203

重點解說

正解 (D)

❸男子說「這間房也是邊間，但它是離樓梯最遠的一間。」farthest 是 far「遠的」最高級，用來說明距離很遠的程度。看圖可得知，公寓 203 是離樓梯最遠的一間，且同樣是邊間，故選項 (D) 為正解。

💡 應試者能理解對話中男子所說的細節並對照圖表，藉此得知男子所敘述的位置。

題目／中文翻譯

Questions 71 through 73 refer to the following announcement.

Attention, passengers on Flight 206 to New York. ❶ This evening's flight has been canceled because of a technical issue. ❷ Please go to the customer service desk in Terminal B, where one of our representatives will assist you with a new reservation. Unfortunately, there are no other outgoing flights to New York tonight, but we will get all of you booked on flights that leave tomorrow morning. ❸ As a courtesy, we've made arrangements for you to stay at the airport hotel tonight.

請參考以下公告，回答第 71 至 73 題。

搭乘 206 班機飛往紐約的乘客請注意。由於技術問題，今晚的班機已取消。請至位於 B 航廈的服務櫃檯，將會有專人協助各位重新訂票。很不幸地，今晚沒有其他飛往紐約的班機，但是我們會幫全體乘客訂好明天早上起飛的班機。為了表示我們的誠意，我們已為各位安排今晚入住機場飯店。

71. Can infer gist, purpose and basic context based on information that is explicitly stated in extended spoken texts

Where are the listeners? | 聽者在哪裡？

(A) At an airport
(B) At a bus terminal
(C) At a train station
(D) At a taxi stand

(A) 機場
(B) 公車轉運站
(C) 火車站
(D) 計程車招呼站

重點解說

正解 (A)
說話者表示❶「由於技術問題，今晚的班機已取消。」在❷也有提到 B 航廈，由此可判斷出聽者是在機場。
technical「技術的」。
(C) station「車站」。
(D) stand「攤位、站」。
💡 應試者能理解生活情境的相關單字，才能聽懂此段公告並推論聽者所在的地點。

72. Can understand details in extended spoken texts

What does the speaker ask the listeners to do? | 說話者要求聽者做什麼？

(A) Present some identification | (A) 出示身分證明
(B) Speak with a representative | **(B) 和專人交談**
(C) Provide a credit card number | (C) 提供信用卡號碼
(D) Weigh some baggage | (D) 將行李稱重

正解 (B)

❷ 提到「請至位於 B 航廈的服務櫃檯，將會有專人協助各位重新訂票。」由此可知，聽者要和服務人員交談，以重新訂票，故選項 (B) 為正解。terminal「航廈、月台、終點站」，representative「代表、代理人」，reservation「預約」。

(A) present「出示」，identification「身分證明」。
(D) weigh「稱重」。

💡 應試者能理解男子所提到的狀況細節。

73. Can understand details in extended spoken texts

What will the listeners receive as a courtesy? | 聽者會得到什麼禮遇？

(A) Hotel accommodations | **(A) 飯店住宿**
(B) Complimentary meals | (B) 免費餐點
(C) Priority seating | (C) 博愛座
(D) Free Internet service | (D) 免費上網服務

正解 (A)

❸ 提到「為了表達我們的誠意，我們已為各位安排今晚入住機場飯店。」句中 arrangements to stay at the airport hotel 與選項 (A) hotel accommodations 意思相近，故為正解。courtesy「禮貌、禮節」，as a courtesy「禮遇」，accommodation「住宿」。

(B) complimentary「免費贈送的」。
(C) priority「優先」。

💡 應試者能理解說話者所說的細節，藉此得知聽者會收到何種禮遇。

Questions 74 through 76 refer to the following announcement.

Before we end our meeting, ❶ I'd like to announce that we're going to have a central air-conditioning system installed. ❷ It's a big investment for a small company like ours, but ultimately it'll make everyone in the office much more comfortable. Anyway, ❸ installation is scheduled for this weekend. It'll require drilling into the ceiling, which will make a bit of a mess. So, ❹ the company that's doing the installation has given us enough plastic sheets to cover everyone's work space. You can pick yours up in the mail room anytime. ❺ Just please remember to cover your desk with it before you leave on Friday.

請參考以下公告，回答第 74 至 76 題。

在我們結束會議之前，我想要宣布一件事，我們即將要安裝中央空調系統。對於我們這樣的小公司而言，這是一筆很大的投資，但最終它會讓辦公室的每個人感到更舒適。總之，安裝工程安排在這個週末。因為需要在天花板上鑽孔，會弄得亂七八糟。因此，進行安裝的公司已提供我們足夠的塑膠布來覆蓋各位的辦公區域，你可以隨時在收發室領取。請記得在週五離開前用它遮蓋好你的辦公桌。

---

74. Can understand details in extended spoken texts

What will be installed this weekend?	本週末將安裝什麼？
(A) Drinking fountains	(A) 飲水機
(B) Videoconferencing equipment	(B) 視訊會議設備
(C) An air-conditioning system	**(C) 空調系統**
(D) An alarm system	(D) 警報系統

重點解說

正解 (C)

說話者提到 ❶「我想要宣布一件事，我們即將要安裝中央空調系統。」接著在 ❸ 提到「安裝工程安排在這個週末」，故選項 (C) 為正解。announce「宣布」，central「中央的」，air-conditioning「空調」。

(A) fountain「噴泉」。

(B) videoconferencing「視訊會議」，equipment「設備」。

(D) alarm「警報」。

💡 應試者能聽懂此段獨白以理解週末將發生的狀況。

75. Can understand details in extended spoken texts

According to the speaker, why is the change being made?

(A) To reduce costs
(B) To increase comfort
(C) To boost productivity
(D) To comply with guidelines

根據說話者所說，做出這項改變的原因為何？

(A) 降低成本
(B) 提升舒適度
(C) 提高生產力
(D) 遵守準則

重點解說

正解 (B)
❷ 提到「對於我們這樣的小公司而言，這是一筆很大的投資，但最終它會讓辦公室的每個人感到更舒適。」句中 much more comfortable 與選項 (B) 的 increase「增加、提升」有相近的意思，故為正解。investment「投資」，ultimately「最終」，comfort「舒適」。
(A) reduce「減少、降低」。
(C) boost「促進、提高」，productivity「生產力」。
(D) comply「遵守」，guideline「準則」。

💡 應試者能理解說話者所提到的狀況細節，藉此得知改變的原因。

---

76. Can understand details in extended spoken texts

What should the listeners do before they leave work on Friday?

(A) Talk to their managers
(B) Move their cars
(C) Cover their desks
(D) Complete a questionnaire

聽者在週五下班前應該做什麼？

(A) 和經理說話
(B) 移動車子
(C) 遮蓋辦公桌
(D) 完成一份問卷

重點解說

正解 (C)
❹ 提到「進行安裝的公司已提供我們足夠的塑膠布來覆蓋各位的辦公區域。」❺ 接著說「記得在週五離開前用它遮蓋好你的辦公桌。」句中的 it 代表 ❹ 提到的塑膠布，故選項 (C) 為正解。installation「安裝」。
(D) questionnaire「問卷、調查表」。

💡 應試者能理解說話者所說的細節，藉此得知聽者該做什麼。

Questions 77 through 79 refer to the following talk.

❶ I called this meeting to demonstrate the new software program we'll be using to manage client contracts. ❷ With this software, you'll be able to create new client accounts, update information quickly, and send contracts by e-mail to be signed electronically. However, ❸ some clients may still request a paper copy of their contract, so please assure them that they'll also receive an official copy in the mail. ❹ We want to switch over to this new software next week. So please pay close attention during the demonstration. I had to read through the manual twice. Let's get started.

請參考以下談話，回答第 77 至 79 題。

我召開這個會議是為了要示範我們即將用於管理客戶合約的新軟體程式。有了這套軟體，你將可以建立新的客戶帳號、迅速地更新資訊、以及透過電子郵件傳送合約並以電子方式簽署。然而，有些客戶也許仍會要求紙本合約，所以請向他們保證，他們也會收到一份郵寄的正式合約。我們想要在下週切換使用這套新軟體，所以請於示範過程中專心學習。我必須將手冊讀過兩次。讓我們開始吧！

77. Can understand details in extended spoken texts

Why has the speaker arranged the meeting?　　說話者為什麼安排了這場會議？

(A) To go over sales data　　(A) 審查銷售數據

(B) To distribute client information　　(B) 分配客戶資訊

(C) To give a demonstration　　**(C) 進行示範**

(D) To assign special projects　　(D) 指派特別項目

重點解說

正解 (C)

說話者說 ❶「我召開這個會議是為了要示範我們即將用於管理客戶合約的新軟體程式。」這代表說話者將要 give a demonstration「進行示範」，故選項 (C) 為正解。demonstrate「示範」，manage「管理」，contract「合約」，arrange「安排」。

(A) data「資料、數據」。

(B) distribute「分發、分配」。

(D) assign「指派」。

💡 應試者能聽懂此段談話以理解說話者安排會議的原因。

78. Can understand details in extended spoken texts

What should the listeners assure clients about?

(A) Orders will be processed on time.
(B) Contracts will be mailed.
(C) Discounts will be applied.
(D) Factory tours will be available.

聽者應該向客戶保證什麼？

(A) 訂單將按時處理。
(B) 將會寄送合約。
(C) 將會使用折扣。
(D) 可以參加工廠導覽。

重點解說

正解 **(B)**

說話者提到❸「有些客戶也許仍會要求紙本合約，所以請向他們保證，他們也會收到一份郵寄的正式合約。」由此可知說話者公司將會用郵寄的方式寄合約給客戶，故選項 (B) 為正解。request「要求」，assure「向…保證、讓…放心」，official「正式的」。
(A) order「訂單」，process「處理」，on time「準時」。
(C) discount「折扣」，apply「使用」。
(D) available「可行的、有空的」。

💡 應試者能理解男子所提到的狀況細節。

79. Can infer gist, purpose and basic context based on information that is explicitly stated in extended spoken texts

Can understand a speaker's purpose or implied meaning in a phrase or sentence

What does the speaker imply when she says, "I had to read through the manual twice"?

(A) A company policy is surprising.
(B) A publication may contain some errors.
(C) A manual was updated.
(D) A software program may be difficult to learn.

說話者說「I had to read through the manual twice」，暗示了什麼？

(A) 公司政策令人驚訝。
(B) 出版物也許出現一些錯誤。
(C) 更新了手冊。
(D) 軟體程式可能不容易學習。

重點解說

正解 **(D)**

說話者說明❷新軟體有許多功能，接著說❹「我們想要在下週切換使用這套新軟體，所以請於示範過程中專心學習。」並在底線部分說明「我必須將手冊讀過兩次。」由此可知，因為新軟體功能多，加上時間緊迫，連說話者在示範前都要重複閱讀手冊，暗指這套軟體可能不容易學習。electronically「電子地」，switch over「切換」，pay attention「注意」，imply「暗示、意味著」，manual「手冊」，twice「兩次」。
(A) policy「政策」。
(B) publication「出版物」，contain「含有」，error「錯誤」。

💡 應試者能從對話中的資訊推論出大意及說話者的意圖。

💡 應試者能理解說話者真正想要表達的意思。

Questions 80 through 82 refer to the following broadcast.

❶ Hello, and welcome to The Money Exchange. ❷ Our guest today is Henry Orton, whose new book, Spend to Save, was just released last week. ❸ In his book, Mr. Orton explains ways to increase the profits of small businesses by investing wisely. This is a topic Mr. Orton has a lot of experience with. ❹ He got his start as the owner of a small stationery store, and he now owns fifteen stationery stores across the country. Today he'll discuss how he did this. Mr. Orton, welcome to the show.

請參考以下廣播，回答第 80 至 82 題。

哈囉，歡迎來到 The Money Exchange 節目。我們今天的來賓是 Henry Orton，他的新書《Spend to Save》上週才剛發表。Orton 先生在他的書中說明透過明智地投資來增加小型企業獲利的方法，這個主題 Orton 先生有許多相關經驗。他從一間小型文具店的老闆開始，如今他在全國擁有 15 間文具店，今天他將說明他是如何辦到的。歡迎 Orton 先生來到節目現場。

80. Can infer gist, purpose and basic context based on information that is explicitly stated in extended spoken texts

What is the radio program mainly about? | 廣播節目的內容主要是關於什麼？

(A) Technology
(B) Finance
(C) Travel
(D) Fitness

(A) 科技
(B) 財經
(C) 旅遊
(D) 健身

重點解說

正解 (B)

說話者於一開頭❶介紹節目名稱為「Money Exchange」，接著在❸提到 Orton 先生在他的書中介紹如何透過明智地投資來增加小型企業的獲利。由此可知此廣播節目的主題與金融相關。exchange「交換」，explain「解釋、說明」，increase「增加」，profit「獲利」，invest「投資」，wisely「明智地」。

💡 應試者能從上下文及相關單字中，聽懂此段廣播並推論此節目所討論的主題。

81. Can understand details in extended spoken texts

According to the speaker, what happened last week?

(A) A company president retired.
(B) A firm celebrated an anniversary.
(C) A mobile application was released.
(D) A new book was published.

根據說話者所說，上週發生什麼事？

(A) 一間公司的總裁退休了。
(B) 一間公司慶祝週年紀念日。
(C) 一款手機應用程式發布了。
(D) 一本新書出版了。

重點解說

正解 **(D)**

說話者介紹節目來賓❷「我們今天的來賓是 Henry Orton，他的新書《Spend to Save》上週才剛發表。」release「發表」，publish「出版」。

(A) president「總裁、董事長」，retire「退休」。

(B) celebrate「慶祝」，anniversary「週年紀念日」。

(C) mobile「手機」，application「應用程式」。

💡 應試者能理解男子所提到的狀況細節。

82. Can understand details in extended spoken texts

What will Mr. Orton be discussing?

(A) How he expanded his business
(B) How to make professional contacts
(C) Ways he stays active
(D) Ways to advertise on social media

Orton 先生將要討論什麼？

(A) 他如何擴展他的事業
(B) 如何建立專業的人脈
(C) 保持活躍的方法
(D) 在社群媒體登廣告的方法

重點解說

正解 **(A)**

主持人提到❹「他從一間小型文具店的老闆開始，如今他在全國擁有 15 間文具店。」由此可知 Orton 先生擴展了他的事業版圖，故選項 (A) 為正解。start「開業、創業」，stationery store「文具店」，across「橫跨」，expand「擴展」。

(B) professional「專業的」，contact「聯繫、熟人」。

(C) active「活躍的」。

(D) advertise「登廣告」，social media「社群媒體」。

💡 應試者能理解說話者所說的細節，藉此得知 Orton 先生要討論的內容。

PART 4

Questions 83 through 85 refer to the following excerpt from a meeting.

Good afternoon, everyone. We're here to discuss plans for a new product. ❶ We've decided to branch out from our successful line of organic juices and add an organic sports drink. The drink will have all-natural ingredients and will come in different fruit flavors. ❷ We conducted a survey and found that 80 percent of our customers prefer beverages made with all-natural ingredients, so we feel confident that they'll buy a new organic drink from us. ❸ We haven't decided on a name for the new product yet. If you have any ideas, please submit them by Friday.

請參考以下會議摘要,回答第 83 至 85 題。

大家午安,我們在這裡是為了討論新產品的計畫。我們已經決定從我們成功的有機果汁系列擴展市場,並加入有機運動飲料。該飲料將會是全天然的成分,並且推出不同的水果口味。公司做了一份問卷調查,結果發現八成的顧客偏好全天然成分製成的飲料,所以我們有信心他們將會從我們這裡購買新的有機飲料。我們尚未決定新產品的名稱,如果你有任何想法,請在週五前提交。

83. | Can infer gist, purpose and basic context based on information that is explicitly stated in extended spoken texts

What has the company decided to do?　　　　這間公司決定要做什麼?

(A) Launch a Web site　　　　　　　　　　(A) 發布網站
(B) Create a new type of beverage　　　**(B) 製造一款新的飲料**
(C) Sell products in vending machines　　　(C) 在販賣機銷售商品
(D) Advertise in sports magazines　　　　　(D) 在運動雜誌登廣告

重點解說

正解 (B)

說話者提到 ❶ 公司打算從現有的有機果汁系列擴展市場到有機運動飲料。選項 (B) 製造一款新的飲料,為正解。branch out「擴展」,organic「有機的」,sports drink「運動飲料」,beverage「飲料」。
(A) launch「發布、啟動」。
(C) vending machine「販賣機」。

💡 應試者能從上下文及相關單字中,聽懂此段摘要並得知這家公司打算做什麼。

---

84. Can understand details in extended spoken texts

What did a survey indicate about customers?

(A) They prefer natural ingredients.
(B) They make online purchases.
(C) They like celebrity promotions.
(D) They want lower prices.

問卷調查說明了關於顧客的什麼事？

(A) 他們偏好天然的成分。
(B) 他們進行網路購物。
(C) 他們喜歡名人促銷活動。
(C) 他們想要更低的價格。

重點解說

正解 (A)

❷說明「公司做了一份問卷調查，結果發現八成的顧客偏好全天然成分製成的飲料。」conduct「進行」，survey「問卷」，prefer「偏好、傾向」，ingredient「成分、材料」。
(B) purchase「購買」。
(C) celebrity「名人、明星」，promotion「宣傳、推銷」。

💡 應試者能理解說話者所提到的狀況細節。

---

85. Can understand details in extended spoken texts

What are the listeners asked to do?

(A) Try a sample
(B) Review a proposal
(C) Submit suggestions
(D) Contact some customers

聽者被要求做什麼？

(A) 試用樣品
(B) 審查企畫書
(C) 提交建議
(D) 聯絡顧客

重點解說

正解 (C)

說話者說❸「我們尚未決定新產品的名稱，如果你有任何想法，請在週五前提交。」由此可知，說話者請聽者集思廣益產品名稱，故選項 (C) 為正解。suggestion「建議」。
(A) sample「樣品」。
(B) proposal「企畫書、提案」。

💡 應試者能理解說話者所說的細節，藉此得知聽者被要求做什麼。

Questions 86 through 88 refer to the following instructions.

Good morning. ❶ Thanks for signing up to volunteer at the annual Mason Health and Wellness Fair. The goal of this year's fair is to increase awareness about maintaining a healthy lifestyle. There'll be a variety of events, including free fitness classes and food preparation demonstrations. ❷ We're expecting a lot more people than last year, so it's going to be really crowded there. I always park behind the bank. ❸ You've signed up to assist with different activities during the health fair, so we'll break off into groups now. Each group will receive special instructions about its responsibilities the day of the fair.

請參考以下指示，回答第 86 至 88 題。

早安。感謝各位自願報名參加一年一度的 Mason 健康與保健博覽會。今年博覽會的目的是要提高人們對保持健康生活方式的意識。博覽會將會有各種活動，包括免費的健身課程以及食物準備的示範。我們預期人數會比去年還要多，所以那裡將會非常擁擠。我總是把車子停在銀行後面。你們已經登記了在健康博覽會期間要協助不同的活動，所以我們現在要分組，每個小組將會收到博覽會當天職責的特別指示。

86. Can understand details in extended spoken texts

What type of event is the speaker discussing?

(A) A health fair
(B) An investment course
(C) A holiday celebration
(D) A restaurant opening

說話者正在討論什麼形式的活動？

(A) 健康博覽會
(B) 投資課程
(C) 節目慶祝活動
(D) 餐廳開業

正解 **(A)**

重點解說

說話者先向與會者說 ❶「感謝各位自願報名參加一年一度的 Mason 健康與保健博覽會。」由此可知選項 (A) 為正解。sign up「報名參加」，annual「年度的」，wellness「健康」，fair「市集、博覽會」。
(B) investment「投資」。
(C) celebration「慶祝」。

💡 應試者能聽懂此段指示以理解活動的類型。

87. Can infer gist, purpose and basic context based on information that is explicitly stated in extended spoken texts

Can understand a speaker's purpose or implied meaning in a phrase or sentence

Why does the speaker say, "I always park behind the bank"?	說話者為什麼說「I always park behind the bank」?
(A) To show surprise	(A) 表達驚訝
(B) To make a complaint	(B) 投訴
(C) To give a recommendation	**(C) 提供建議**
(D) To correct a mistake	(D) 糾正錯誤

正解 (C)

說話者說明❷「我們預期人數會比去年還要多,所以那裡將會非常擁擠。」底線部分表示「我總是把車子停在銀行後面」,由此可知,說話者希望志工們在停車時避開車潮。因此他是在提供志工們停車位置的建議。

(B) complaint「抱怨、不滿」。

💡 應試者能從對話中的資訊推論出大意及說話者的意圖。

💡 應試者能理解說話者真正想要表達的意思。

88. Can understand details in extended spoken texts

What will the listeners do next?	聽者接下來會做什麼?
(A) Look at a map	(A) 看地圖
(B) Watch a film	(B) 看電影
(C) Update a calendar	(C) 更新行事曆
(D) Divide into groups	**(D) 分組**

正解 (D)

❸提到這些志工都將在博覽會協助不同活動,所以要將他們分組。句中的 break off「分開」指的就是選項 (D) 中的 divide「分開」,故為正解。

(C) calendar「行事曆」。

💡 應試者能理解說話者所說的細節,藉此得知聽者接下來將會做什麼。

Questions 89 through 91 refer to the following telephone message.

Hi, Stella. This is Marco. It's about five thirty, and I'm just leaving the office supply store on Tenth Street. ❶ They have the keyboards we're looking for, but, unfortunately, the computer cables we need are sold-out. But ❷ they're available at their other store location across town. That store closes at six, and it's pretty far from here. I don't think it will delay our work if I pick them up tomorrow. By the way, ❸ I forgot to follow up with the job candidate we selected. Could you call and schedule her to interview next Monday?

請參考以下電話留言,回答第 89 至 81 題。

嗨,Stella,我是 Marco。現在大約五點半,而我正要離開位在第十街的辦公用品店。它們有我們在找的鍵盤,但可惜我們需要的電腦線賣完了。不過他們在城鎮另一端的店面還有貨,那間店六點關門,而且離這裡相當遠。我認為如果我明天去拿這兩樣東西,也不會延誤到我們的工作。順帶一提,我忘了跟進我們選出的應徵者。你可以打電話給她並安排她下週一面試嗎?

89. Can infer gist, purpose and basic context based on information that is explicitly stated in extended spoken texts

What is the speaker shopping for?　　　　說話者要買什麼東西?

(A) Groceries　　　　　　　　　　　　(A) 食品雜貨
(B) Kitchen appliances　　　　　　　　(B) 廚房用具
(C) Sporting goods　　　　　　　　　　(C) 運動用品
(D) Computer accessories　　　　　**(D) 電腦配件**

重
點
解
說

正解 (D)

說話者說 ❶「它們有我們在找的鍵盤,但可惜我們需要的電腦線賣完了。」說話者提到鍵盤和電腦線,由此可推知他在購買電腦配件。keyboard「鍵盤」,look for「尋找」, unfortunately「可惜」,cable「電線」,sold-out「售完」,accessory「配件」。

(B) appliance「用具、設備」。

💡 應試者能從上下文及相關單字中,聽懂此段電話留言並推論說話者購買的商品類型。

90.

What does the speaker mean when he says, "it's pretty far from here"?

(A) He is unable to complete a task today.
(B) He will need to borrow a car.
(C) He may be late for an appointment.
(D) He needs driving directions.

說話者說「it's pretty far from here」是什麼意思？

(A) 他今天無法完成任務。
(B) 他需要借一輛車。
(C) 他的約會可能會遲到。
(D) 他需要行車導航。

重點解說

正解 (A)

男子一開頭提及目前時間約為五點半，接著 ❷ 說明他們在城鎮另一端的店面還有貨，但那間店六點關門。底線部分補充說明「那間店離這裡相當遠」，暗指說話者認為他無法在六點前抵達那間店面，表示他今天無法完成任務。unable「無法」，complete「完成」。
(B) borrow「借」。
(C) appointment「約會、預約」。
(D) direction「方向」。

💡 應試者能從對話中的資訊推論出大意及說話者的意圖。

💡 應試者能理解說話者真正想要表達的意思。

91.

What does the speaker ask the listener to do?

(A) Print a document
(B) Address some letters
(C) Arrange an interview
(D) Process a refund

說話者要求聽者做什麼？

(A) 列印文件
(B) 寫信
(C) 安排面試
(D) 處理退款

重點解說

正解 (C)

說話者說 ❸ 他忘了後續安排跟之前選出的應徵者進行面試，想請聽者與對方聯繫，故選項 (C) 為正解。follow up「跟進」，candidate「應徵者、候選人」，arrange「安排」。
(A) document「文件」。
(B) address「寫上姓名（或地址）」。
(D) process「處理」，refund「退款、退費」。

💡 應試者能理解說話者所說的細節，藉此得知他要聽者做什麼。

Questions 92 through 94 refer to the following broadcast.

❶ This is Active Wear Daily, a podcast show where I try out different types of exercise clothes and review them for my listeners. But before I begin, I wanted to apologize for how my Web site looks. ❷ The layout redesign has taken longer than expected, but the project should be done soon. Now, in this episode, I'm going to talk about a line of jackets by the company Fayton. ❸ Last week I tried one when I participated in a ten-kilometer race on a cool morning, and it kept me very warm. And I won a silver medal!

請參考以下廣播，回答第 92 至 94 題。

這裡是 Podcast 節目《Active Wear Daily 》，我在節目中嘗試不同類型的運動服裝，並為我的聽眾寫評論。但是在開始之前，我想為我網站呈現的樣子道歉。重新設計版型比預期花了更久的時間，但這個專案應該很快就會完成。現在，在這一集中，我將會討論 Fayton 公司的夾克系列。上週我在一個涼爽的早晨參加一場十公里比賽時試穿了其中一件夾克，它讓我非常溫暖。而且我贏得了銀牌！

92. | Can understand details in extended spoken texts

What type of products does the speaker review? | 說話者要評論什麼類型的產品？

(A) Home furniture
(B) Video games
(C) Cosmetics
(D) Exercise clothing

(A) 家用家具
(B) 電玩遊戲
(C) 化妝品
(D) 運動服飾

重點解說

正解 (D)
❶ 說話者先介紹播客節目名稱為 Active Wear Daily，active wear 指的是運動時所穿著的服飾，說話者接著也說明他將在節目中試穿及評論不同類型的運動服飾。try out「試用」。
(A) furniture「家具」。
💡 應試者能聽懂此段廣播以理解說話者評論何種產品。

93. `Can understand details in extended spoken texts`

Why does the speaker apologize?

(A) A description was incorrect.
(B) A guest has canceled.
(C) A sponsor has withdrawn.
(D) A project has been delayed.

說話者為什麼要道歉？

(A) 描述有誤。
(B) 來賓已取消。
(C) 贊助商退出。
(D) 計畫延遲。

重點解說

正解 (D)

說話者先說他要為他網站的外觀道歉，接著❷說明「重新設計版型比預期花了更久的時間，但這個專案應該很快就會完成。」由此可知，因所花的時間超出預期，代表計畫延遲。layout「版型，版面配置」，expect「預期」。delay「延遲」。

(A) description「描述」，incorrect「不正確」。
(B) cancel「取消」。
(C) sponsor「贊助商」，withdraw「退出、撤銷」。

💡 應試者能理解說話者所說的細節，藉此得知說話者為什麼要道歉。

94. `Can understand details in extended spoken texts`

What activity did the speaker participate in last week?

(A) A competition
(B) A fashion show
(C) A fund-raiser
(D) A community festival

說話者上週參加什麼活動？

(A) 比賽
(B) 時裝秀
(C) 募款活動
(D) 社區節慶

重點解說

正解 (A)

說話者說❸「上週我在一個涼爽的早晨參加一場十公里比賽時試穿了其中一件夾克。」選項 (A) competition 也有比賽之意，故為正解。participate in「參加」，race「比賽」。

(C) fund-raiser「募款活動」。
(D) community「社區、團體」，festival「節日」。

💡 應試者能理解說話者所說的細節，藉此得知他上週參與什麼活動。

Questions 95 through 97 refer to the following tour information and map.

Welcome to Kinbridge Farm! Today I'll show you around the grounds and tell you about how things are run here. First we'll go to the beehives, where the famous Kinbridge honey is produced. ❶ We won't be stopping at the cornfield—the corn-growing season is now over, and the field's closed. So next we'll go to the orchard, where our apples are in season. ❷ You'll be able to fill your complimentary bag with apples—free with your tour—as I explain our different varieties. Oh, ❸ and don't forget that we have a farm store where you can buy our wonderful products at the end of the tour.

請參考以下旅遊資訊和地圖,回答第 95 至 97 題。

歡迎來到 Kinbridge 農場!今天我將帶領你們參觀這個園區,並且告訴你們這個地方是如何運作。首先我們將前往生產著名的 Kinbridge 蜂蜜的蜂箱。我們不會在玉米田停留,因玉米種植的季節已經結束,該區已關閉。下一站我們會去到果園,現在正值蘋果產季。當我講解我們不同的品種時,你們可以免費將附贈的袋子裝滿蘋果。喔,別忘了我們還有農場商店,各位可在參觀結束時前往購買我們的優質商品。

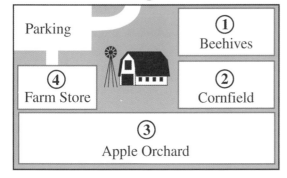

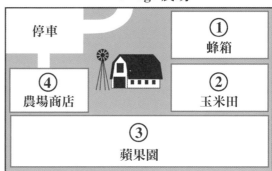

95. Can understand details in extended spoken texts

Look at the graphic. What area is currently closed?

(A) Area 1
(B) Area 2
(C) Area 3
(D) Area 4

請看圖,哪一個區域目前關閉?

(A) 區域 1
(B) 區域 2
(C) 區域 3
(D) 區域 4

重點解說

正解 (B)

說話者說明不在玉米田停留的原因❶「我們不會在玉米田停留,因玉米種植的季節已經結束,該區已關閉。」由此可知關閉的區域是玉米田,對照圖表玉米田在 2 號區域。cornfield「玉米田」,field「田、地、牧場」。

💡 應試者能理解此段旅遊資訊並對照圖表,以得知哪個區域目前關閉。

96. Can understand details in extended spoken texts

According to the speaker, what will the listeners receive?

(A) Homemade cookies
(B) A discount coupon
(C) A bottle of water
(D) Free fruit

根據說話者，聽者將會收到什麼？

(A) 手工餅乾
(B) 優惠券
(C) 一瓶水
(D) 免費水果

重點解說

正解 (D)

說話者說明❷「你們可以免費將附贈的袋子裝滿蘋果。一參加導覽就免費。」由此可知入園參觀的人都能有免費的水果，故選項 (D) 為正解。be able to「能夠」，complimentary「（由公司）免費贈送的」。
(A) homemade「家裡自製的、手工的」。
(B) coupon「優惠券」。
(C) a bottle of「一瓶」。

💡 應試者能理解旅遊資訊中說話者所提到的狀況細節。

97. Can understand details in extended spoken texts

What does the speaker remind the listeners about?

(A) What equipment to bring
(B) When to return to the parking area
(C) Where to buy some goods
(D) Who sponsored the tour

說話者提醒聽者什麼事？

(A) 需要攜帶的設備
(B) 要回到停車區的時間
(C) 買商品的地方
(D) 贊助導覽的人

重點解說

正解 (C)

說話者說❸「別忘了我們還有農場商店，各位可在參觀結束時前往購買我們的優質商品。」句中的 don't forget 通常用於提醒他人。由此可知，他提醒聽者購買商品的地方。選項 (C) goods「商品、貨物」與句中的 products 意思相同，故為正解。remind「提醒」。
(A) equipment「設備、器材」。
(B) return「返回」。
(D) sponsor「資助、贊助」。

💡 應試者能理解說話者所說的細節，藉此得知他提醒聽者何事。

Questions 98 through 100 refer to the following telephone message and schedule.

Hi, Louise. I met with the marketing manager at Kumar Construction this morning. Great news! They want our company to design their new Web site. ❶ I'm concerned, though, because we have so many new people on staff right now who have little experience. This would be their first big Web-design project. Mr. Kumar, the owner, wants to discuss a design with us next week, but you and I should meet before then. ❷ Let's get together after the directors' strategy meeting, in the afternoon. Also, could you do me a favor? ❸ Could you look at the budget for this project? I need to submit it for approval by the end of the week. Thanks.

請參考以下電話留言和行程表，回答第 98 至 100 題。

嗨，Louise，今天早上我和 Kumar 建設的行銷經理見面。好消息！他們希望由我們公司設計他們的新網站。但是我有點擔心，因為我們有太多經驗不足的新進員工，這將是他們的第一個大型網頁設計案子。老闆 Kumar 先生下週想和我們討論設計方案，但是你和我應該在那之前先見個面。我們在下午主管策略會議結束後來開個會。另外，你可以幫我一個忙嗎？你能看一下這個案子的預算嗎？我需要在這週結束前提交以供核準。謝謝。

	Mon.	Tues.	Wed.	Thurs.
8:00	Planning meeting			
9:00		Work on budget report	Leadership training	Finish budget report
10:00	Presentation		Directors' strategy meeting	
1:00		Team meeting		

	週一	週二	週三	週四
8:00	計畫會議			
9:00		處理預算報告	領導能力訓練	完成預算報告
10:00	報告		主管策略會議	
1:00		小組會議		

98. Can understand details in extended spoken texts

What is the speaker concerned about?

(A) A short timeline
(B) An advertising campaign
(C) Technical issues
(D) Inexperienced staff

說話者擔心什麼？

(A) 時程很短
(B) 廣告行銷活動
(C) 技術問題
(D) 經驗不足的員工

重點解說

正解 (D)

說話者說 ❶「但是我有點擔心，因為我們有太多經驗不足的新進員工。」選項 (D) inexperienced「沒有經驗的」同樣也是說明員工的工作經驗很少。concern「擔心」。
(A) timeline「時程」。
(B) advertise「登廣告」，campaign「行銷活動」。
(C) technical「技術的」，issue「問題」。

💡 應試者能理解此段電話留言以理解說話者擔心的事情。

99. Can understand details in extended spoken texts

Look at the graphic. When does the speaker suggest meeting?

(A) On Monday
(B) On Tuesday
(C) On Wednesday
(D) On Thursday

請看圖，說話者建議什麼時候開會？

(A) 週一
(B) 週二
(C) 週三
(D) 週四

> **重點解說**
>
> 正解 (C)
>
> 說話者建議❷「我們在下午主管策略會議結束後來開個會。」根據圖表，主管策略會議在週三。director「主管」，strategy「策略」。
>
> 💡 應試者能理解說話者所提到的狀況細節，並對照圖表選出建議開會的時間。

100. Can understand details in extended spoken texts

What does the speaker ask the listener to do?

(A) Finalize a construction schedule
(B) Review a budget
(C) Create a meeting agenda
(D) Call a potential client

說話者請求聽者做什麼？

(A) 敲定施工行程
(B) 審核預算
(C) 建立會議議程
(D) 致電給潛在客戶

> **重點解說**
>
> 正解 (B)
>
> 說話者說❸「你能看一下這個案子的預算嗎？我需要在這週結束前提交以供核準。」由此可以推測說話者需要聽者審閱一份預算表。submit「提交」，approval「許可、批准」。
> (A) finalize「敲定」，construction「施工」，schedule「行程、進度」。
> (C) agenda「議程」。
> (D) potential「潛在的」，client「客戶」。
>
> 💡 應試者能理解說話者所說的細節，藉此得知說話者請聽者做的事情。

題目/中文翻譯

1. ▏Can infer gist, purpose and basic context based on information that is explicitly stated in short spoken texts

(A) She's running in a park.

(B) She's putting on boots.

(C) She's pushing a wheelbarrow.

(D) She's filling a bucket.

(A) 她正在公園裡跑步。

(B) 她正在穿上靴子。

(C) 她正推著獨輪手推車。

(D) 她正在填滿一個水桶。

正解 (C)

女子正推著獨輪手推車。wheelbarrow「獨輪手推車」。

(A) 女子沒有正在公園跑步。

(B) 女子沒有正在穿靴子。put on「穿」，boots「靴子」。

(D) 圖片中的獨輪手推車上雖然有個桶子，但女子並沒有正在填滿桶子。bucket「桶子」。

💡 應試者能理解圖片中人物的動作和物品的單字，從中將正確的語句與圖片配對。

---

2. ▏Can understand details in short spoken texts

(A) They're installing a photocopier.

(B) They're replacing a window.

(C) One of the men is hanging a sign.

(D) One of the men is reaching for a telephone.

(A) 他們正在安裝一台影印機。

(B) 他們正在更換一扇窗戶。

(C) 其中一位男子正在掛牌子。

(D) 其中一位男子正要伸手去拿電話。

正解 (D)

左邊男子正要伸手拿電話，右邊男子則是站在電腦前。reach for「伸手拿（東西）」。

(A) 兩位男子皆沒有在安裝影印機。install「安裝」，photocopier「影印機」。

(B) 雖然圖中有扇窗戶，但兩位男子皆沒有在更換窗戶。replace「更換」。

(C) 兩位男子皆沒有在掛牌子。hang「掛、吊」，sign「標誌、牌子」。

💡 應試者能理解圖片及選項中所提到的動作和物品的單字，並將正確的語句與圖片配對。

題目／中文翻譯

3. Can infer gist, purpose and basic context based on information that is explicitly stated in short spoken texts

(A) He's removing an item from a bag.
(B) He's carrying a tray of food.
(C) He's giving money to a cashier.
(D) He's drinking from a bottle of water.

(A) 他正從袋子裡拿出一樣物品。
(B) 他正端著一盤食物。
(C) 他正在付錢給收銀員。
(D) 他正在喝一瓶水。

正解 (A)

重點解說

男子正從袋子裡拿出物品。remove...from「從⋯移除」，item「物品」。
(B) 桌上有托盤，但男子沒有端著托盤。carry「端、提」，tray「托盤、盤子」。
(C) 男子沒有正在付錢給收銀員，且圖片中也沒有收銀員。cashier「收銀員」。
(D) 桌上有一瓶水，但男子並沒有在喝水。

💡 應試者能理解圖片中人物的動作和物品的單字，從中將正確的語句與圖片配對。

4. Can understand details in short spoken texts

(A) The woman is using a broom.
(B) The woman is trying on a helmet.
(C) The man is measuring a cabinet.
(D) The man is painting a wall.

(A) 女子正在使用掃把。
(B) 女子正在試戴安全帽。
(C) 男子正在測量櫃子。
(D) 男子正在粉刷一面牆。

正解 (B)

重點解說

女子正在試戴安全帽。try on「試穿、試戴」，helmet「頭盔、安全帽」。
(A) 女子沒有在使用掃把。broom「掃把」。
(C) 圖中雖然有櫃子，但男子沒有在測量櫃子。measure「測量」，cabinet「櫃子」。
(D) 男子沒有在粉刷牆壁。paint「粉刷」。

💡 應試者能理解圖片的內容，以及句子中提到的動作和物品的單字，並將正確的語句與圖片配對。

5. Can infer gist, purpose and basic context based on information that is explicitly stated in short spoken texts

(A) The women are shaking hands.
(B) The women are facing each other.
(C) One of the women is sipping from a cup.
(D) One of the women is stapling a document.

(A) 女子們正在握手。
(B) 女子們正面對面。
(C) 其中一位女子正從杯子裡啜飲。
(D) 其中一位女子正在裝訂文件。

正解 (B)

重點解說

兩位女子正面對著彼此。face 在此作為動詞，意思是從其正對面看向一個特定的方向，為「面對」的意思。
(A) 雖然都有看到兩位女子的手，但她們沒有在握手。shake hands「握手」。
(C) 兩位女子皆沒有在啜飲。sip「啜飲」。
(D) 桌上雖然有看到釘書機，但沒有人在裝訂文件。staple「裝訂」，document「文件」。

💡 應試者能理解圖片中人物的動作和物品的單字，從中將正確的語句與圖片配對。

6. Can understand details in short spoken texts

(A) A kayak is being paddled down a river.
(B) A pile of bricks has been left on a walkway.
(C) Some roofs are being repaired.
(D) Some chairs have been placed along a canal.

(A) 一艘獨木舟正順著河流划動。
(B) 一堆的磚頭被留在走道上。
(C) 有一些屋頂正在整修中。
(D) 沿著運河有擺放一些椅子。

正解 (D)

重點解說

沿著運河有擺放一些椅子。選項 (D) 的 place 在此作動詞，意思是將某物放在一個特定位置，為「擺放」的意思。along「沿著」，canal「運河」。
(A) 圖片中沒有看到獨木舟，也沒有人正順著河流划動獨木舟。kayak「獨木舟」，paddle「用槳划船」。
(B) 走道上並沒有看到一堆磚塊。a pile of「一堆」，brick「磚塊」，walkway「走道」。
(C) 圖片中沒有任何線索顯示屋頂在整修中。repair「整修」。

💡 應試者能理解圖片的內容，以及句子中提到的動作和物品的單字，並將正確的語句與圖片配對。

題目/中文翻譯

7. Can understand details in short spoken texts

How many packages did your company ship last month?

(A) No, I don't need any.
(B) You can take the bus to the port.
(C) About 5,000.

上個月你們公司運送了多少件包裹？

(A) 不，我不需要任何東西。
(B) 你可以搭公車前往港口。
(C) 大約 5,000 件。

正解 (C)

重點解說

「How many...?」通常用來詢問數字。這題是詢問包裹運送的數量，選項 (C) 具體說明約有 5,000 件，故為正解。ship 在此是作為動詞「運送」的意思。
(A) 題目未詢問是否需要什麼。
(B) port「港口」看似與 ship 有關，但題目中的 ship 為動詞，非名詞「大船」的意思，故答非所問。

💡 應試者能理解問題詢問意圖，並選出適當的回應。

8. Can understand details in short spoken texts

Who ordered the side salad?

(A) A fork and knife.
(B) By credit card.
(C) That was me.

誰點了配菜沙拉？

(A) 一把刀和叉子。
(B) 用信用卡。
(C) 是我。

正解 (C)

重點解說

「Who...?」通常用來詢問人物。這題詢問是誰點了配菜沙拉，選項 (C) 明確回應點餐的人，故為正解。side「配菜」。
(A) fork「叉子」，knife「刀子」，但題目與餐具無關。
(B) by 在此是「用何種方式」的意思，但題目並未詢問付費方式。

💡 應試者能理解問題詢問意圖，並選出適當的回應。

9. Can understand a speaker's purpose or implied meaning in a phrase or sentence

Where's Dr. Mattison's office?

(A) Because it's raining.
(B) There's a directory in the lobby.
(C) It starts at two o'clock.

Mattison 博士的辦公室在哪裡？

(A) 因為正在下雨。
(B) 在大廳裡有一個指南。
(C) 兩點開始。

正解 (B)

重點解說

「Where...?」通常用來詢問位置。這題詢問 Mattison 博士辦公室的位置，選項 (B) 雖沒有直接回答確切地點，但提到大廳裡有指南，暗指可以參考指南找到博士的辦公室，是最為合理的答案。directory「指南」，lobby「大廳」。
(A) 題目未詢問原因。
(C) 題目未詢問時間。

💡 應試者能理解問題詢問意圖，即使選項是以間接或隱含的方式回答。

10. Can understand details in short spoken texts

Have you seen the new film at the cinema yet?

(A) No, I'm going to go see it tomorrow.
(B) An award-winning movie director.
(C) To visit my friend.

你去電影院看這部新上映的電影了嗎？

(A) 不，我明天會去看。
(B) 一個獲獎的電影導演。
(C) 去拜訪我的朋友。

重點解說

正解 (A)

現在完成式疑問句「Have you +過去分詞 ...yet?」通常用來詢問過去的經驗。這題詢問對方是否已去電影院看過新上映的電影，選項 (A) 回答者以否定 no 回答，並接著表示要去看電影的時間，故為正解。seen 為 see 的過去分詞，film「電影」，cinema「電影院」。
(B) award-winning「獲獎的」，director「導演」，與題目中的 film 相關，但題目並非詢問人物。
(C) 題目與拜訪朋友無關。

💡 應試者能理解問題詢問重點，並選出適當的回應。

11. Can understand details in short spoken texts

When did they announce Barbara's promotion to vice president?

(A) A hard worker.
(B) On Monday.
(C) Yes, she is.

他們什麼時候公告 Barbara 升職為副總裁？

(A) 一個努力工作的人。
(B) 星期一。
(C) 是的，她是。

重點解說

正解 (B)

「When...?」通常詢問時間。這題詢問何時公告 Barbara 升職為副總裁的消息，選項 (B) 明確說明時間，故為正解。announce「宣布、公告」，promotion「升遷」，vice president「副總裁、副總經理」。
(A) 題目並未詢問員工工作狀態。
(C) 題目詢問時間，回答 yes 或 no 皆答非所問。

💡 應試者能理解問題詢問意圖，並選出適當的回應。

12. Can understand a speaker's purpose or implied meaning in a phrase or sentence

Could I discuss the budget proposal with you later today?

(A) Twenty copies, please.
(B) I'll be leaving early.
(C) That can't be right.

今天稍晚的時候我可以和你討論預算提案嗎？

(A) 20 份影本，麻煩了。
(B) 我會提早離開。
(C) 那不可能是對的。

重點解說

正解 (B)

通常助動詞「Could I...?」為開頭的問句，要用 Yes／No 回答。題目詢問是否可於今天稍晚的時候與對方討論預算提案，選項 (B) 雖然沒有直接回答，但告知對方「我會提早離開」，暗指今天稍晚的時間沒辦法討論。
(A) 題目並未詢問影印數量。
(C) 題目詢問對方是否有空，回答「那不可能是對的」為答非所問。

💡 應試者能理解問題詢問意圖，即使選項是以間接或隱含的方式回答。

13. Can understand details in short spoken texts

Do we need to take a number, or can we just get in line? | 我們需要拿一張號碼牌，還是我們可以直接排隊？

(A) We can get in line. | **(A) 我們可以排隊。**
(B) I didn't count them. | (B) 我沒有算他們。
(C) Sure, I'll buy it for you. | (C) 當然，我可以買給你。

重點解說

正解 (A)

「A or B?」句型詢問需要拿號碼牌或可以直接排隊，選項 (A) 明確回答可以直接排隊，為最合理的答案。get in line「排隊」。
(B) count「計算」雖與 number 有關，但題目未詢問是否有計算數量。
(C) 題目未詢問是否可以為其購買。

💡 應試者能理解問題詢問重點，並選出適當的回應。

14. Can understand details in short spoken texts

Your suitcase is new, isn't it? | 你的手提箱是新的，是吧？

(A) The baggage counter. | (A) 行李櫃檯。
(B) Just a suit and tie. | (B) 只有一套西裝和領帶。
(C) No, it's not. | **(C) 不，它不是。**

重點解說

正解 (C)

像「..., isn't it?」這類的附加問句，通常是用來與對方確認某事是否是對的，或是尋求對方同意。這題是用來與對方再次確認手提箱是否為新的，此句型要用 Yes／No 回答，故選項 (C) 為最適切的答案。suitcase「手提箱」。
(A) baggage「行李」與 counter「櫃檯」雖看似與題目 suitcase 有關，但答非所問。
(B) 雖然套裝和領帶可以放入手提箱中，但這題與衣物無關。suit「套裝」，tie「領帶」。

💡 應試者能理解問題詢問重點，並選出適當的回應。

15. Can understand details in short spoken texts

Wasn't Mr. Keller supposed to come to this business dinner? | Keller 先生不是應該會來這場商務晚宴嗎？

(A) Recruiting strategies. | (A) 招募策略。
(B) Yes, he'll be here in ten minutes. | **(B) 是的，他將會在 10 分鐘內抵達。**
(C) Would you prefer chicken? | (C) 你比較喜歡雞肉嗎？

重點解說

正解 (B)

否定疑問句通常用來確認肯定或否定的想法。這題用來確認「Keller 先生是否應該會來這場商務晚宴」，表示問話者認為 Keller 先生應該出席晚宴。否定疑問句通常要用 Yes／No 回答。選項 (B) 除了以 yes 開頭外，也補充說明 Keller 先生會在 10 分鐘內抵達。supposed to＋V「應該做…」。
(A) recruit「招募」與 strategy「策略」雖看似與題目中的 business 有關，但題目並未提到招募相關內容。
(C) 「Would you prefer N／Ving?」用來詢問對方偏好，題目雖然是關於晚餐，但並未詢問飲食偏好。

💡 應試者能理解問題詢問重點，並選出適當的回應。

TEST 2

16. Can infer gist, purpose and basic context based on information that is explicitly stated in short spoken texts

Can understand a speaker's purpose or implied meaning in a phrase or sentence

Who can pick up Mr. Park from the airport?

(A) I don't have a car.
(B) A one-way ticket.
(C) Yes, it's pretty heavy.

誰可以去機場接 Park 先生？

(A) 我沒有車。
(B) 一張單程票。
(C) 是的，它相當重。

正解 (A)

重點解說

「Who..?」通常是用來詢問人物。這題詢問誰可以去機場接 Park 先生，選項 (A) 回答「我沒有車。」由此可推斷回答者無法去機場接 Park 先生，因需要有車子才能做此事。pick up「接某人」。
(B) 雖然 one-way ticket「單程票」與機場和航空公司有關，但題目與票種無關。
(C) 題目未詢問重量。pretty 用來形容副詞或形容詞的程度「相當」。

💡 應試者能推斷說話者的目的。

💡 即使說話者沒有直接回應或回應內容難以預測，應試者仍能理解說話者真正想表達的含意。

17. Can understand details in short spoken texts

Where did the accounting department move to?

(A) I work in that department, too.
(B) The company's bank account.
(C) Right across the hall.

會計部搬到哪裡？

(A) 我也在那個部門工作。
(B) 公司的銀行帳戶。
(C) 就在大廳對面。

正解 (C)

重點解說

「Where...?」通常詢問位置。這題詢問會計部搬到哪裡，選項 (C) 明確說明位置「就在大廳對面」，故為正解。accounting department「會計部」。
(A) 題目未詢問對方在哪個部門工作。
(B) bank account「銀行帳戶」與 accounting department 看似相關，但題目未詢問是何種帳戶。

💡 應試者能理解問題詢問重點，並選出適當的回應。

18. Can understand details in short spoken texts

Does this mobile phone come with headphones?

(A) Yes, it does.
(B) Thanks, I'm fine.
(C) About two days.

這款手機有附耳機嗎？

(A) 是的，它有。
(B) 謝謝，我很好。
(C) 大約兩天。

正解 (A)

重點解說

這是一個用助動詞 Do／Does 開頭的典型問句，通常此類問題會以 Yes／No 回答。這題詢問手機是否有附耳機，選項 (A) 先以 yes 開頭回答，而 it 指的就是 mobile phone，故為正解。come with「附帶」，headphones「耳機」。
(B) 題目未詢問對方是否需要協助。
(C) 題目與時間長度無關。

💡 應試者能理解問題詢問重點，並選出適當的回應。

19. Can understand details in short spoken texts

Why are production numbers so low this month?

(A) One meter high.
(B) Because some machines were down for repairs.
(C) A few hundred units.

為什麼這個月的生產量這麼低？

(A) 一公尺高。
(B) 因為有一些機器故障送修。
(C) 幾百個單位。

> **正解 (B)**
> 「Why...?」詢問為何這個月的生產量很低，選項 (B) 明確說明原因「因為有些機器故障送修」，故為正解。down 「停止運作的」，repair「維修」。
> (A) high 與 low 相關，但題目未詢問高度。meter「公尺」。
> (C) 題目並未詢問數量。
> 💡 應試者能理解問題詢問重點，並選出適當的回應。

20. Can understand details in short spoken texts

You're going to the office picnic, aren't you?

(A) Ms. Cho, the head of marketing.
(B) Yes, I'll be there.
(C) A large catering order.

你要去辦公室的野餐，是吧？

(A) Cho 小姐，行銷部主管。
(B) 是的，我會去。
(C) 一筆大的外燴訂單。

> **正解 (B)**
> 肯定句最後加上「..., aren't you?」表示「…是吧？」再次確認對方是否會參加公司野餐，選項 (B) 回答「會，我會去。」最為適合。
> (A) 題目未詢問職務。head of marketing「行銷部主管」。
> (C) catering「外燴」與 picnic 看似有關，但答非所問。
> 💡 應試者能理解問題詢問意圖，並選出適當的回應。

21. Can infer gist, purpose and basic context based on information that is explicitly stated in short spoken texts

Can understand a speaker's purpose or implied meaning in a phrase or sentence

How much does this watch cost?

(A) Not very often these days.
(B) It's quarter to eleven.
(C) Is the price tag missing?

這支手錶多少錢？

(A) 這幾天不常。
(B) 現在是10:45。
(C) 價格標籤不見了嗎？

> **正解 (C)**
> 「How much...?」詢問手錶的價格，選項 (C) 回問「價格標籤不見了嗎？」暗指可以先看價格標籤。
> (A) 題目未詢問頻率。
> (B) 題目問的是價格而非時間。
> 💡 應試者能推斷說話者的目的。
> 💡 即使說話者沒有直接回應或回應內容難以預測，應試者仍能理解說話者真正想表達的含意。

TEST 2

22. Can infer gist, purpose and basic context based on information that is explicitly stated in short spoken texts

Can understand a speaker's purpose or implied meaning in a phrase or sentence

When does the reception start?

(A) On Barton Avenue.
(B) I didn't receive an invitation.
(C) Seventy guests.

接待處何時開始？

(A) 在 Barton 大道。
(B) 我沒有收到邀請函。
(C) 70 位客人。

重點解說

正解 **(B)**

「When...?」詢問接待處何時開始，選項 (B) 回答「我沒有收到邀請函。」暗指不清楚幾點開始。reception「接待處」，receive「收到」，invitation「邀請函」。
(A) 題目未詢問地點。
(C) 題目未詢問參加招待會的人數。

💡 應試者能推斷說話者的目的。

💡 即使說話者沒有直接回應或回答內容難以預測，應試者仍能理解說話者真正想表達的含意。

23. Can infer gist, purpose and basic context based on information that is explicitly stated in short spoken texts

Can understand a speaker's purpose or implied meaning in a phrase or sentence

Which software programs does Allison know how to use?

(A) Here's a copy of her résumé.
(B) That's my computer.
(C) Some technical consultants.

Allison 會使用哪個軟體程式？

(A) 這是她的履歷影本。
(B) 那是我的電腦。
(C) 一些技術顧問。

重點解說

正解 **(A)**

「Which...?」詢問 Allison 會使用哪個軟體程式，選項 (A) 回答「這是她的履歷影本。」暗指詢問的人可以直接看 Allison 的履歷，並從中找到答案。
(B) computer 與 software programs 有關，但答非所問。
(C) 題目與 technical consultant「技術顧問」無關，此為答非所問。

💡 應試者能推斷說話者的目的。

💡 即使說話者沒有直接回應或回應內容難以預測，應試者仍能理解說話者真正想表達的含意。

24. Can infer gist, purpose and basic context based on information that is explicitly stated in short spoken texts

Can understand a speaker's purpose or implied meaning in a phrase or sentence

I don't know how to get to the convention center from the airport.

(A) Satoshi's printing out the directions.
(B) A complimentary breakfast.
(C) A thousand people attended.

我不知道如何從機場到會議中心。

(A) Satoshi 正在列印路線指示。
(B) 一頓免費的早餐。
(C) 有 1000 個人參加。

重點解說

正解 **(A)**

說話者說「我不知道如何從機場到會議中心。」選項 (A) 回答「Satoshi 正在列印路線指示。」表示到時可以參考路線指示。convention center「會議中心」，print out「印出」，direction「路線指示」。
(B) 題目與附贈的早餐無關。complimentary「免費贈送的」。
(C) 題目並未詢問人數。

💡 應試者能推斷說話者的目的。

💡 即使說話者沒有直接回應或回應內容難以預測，應試者仍能理解說話者真正想表達的含意。

25. Can understand details in short spoken texts

Why don't you type up the meeting report and e-mail it to the team?

(A) From two thirty to five o'clock.
(B) A presentation on market expansion.
(C) Sure—I'll do it immediately.

你何不將會議報告打字出來並以電子郵件寄給團隊呢？

(A) 從兩點半到五點。
(B) 市場拓展的簡報。
(C) 沒問題，我會馬上做。

> **正解 (C)**
>
> 「Why don't you...?」句型給予對方建議，可將會議報告打字出來並以電子郵件方式寄給整個團隊。選項 (C) 回答 sure，並接著說明「我會馬上做」，it 代表題目建議的做法。type up「把手寫的打出來」，immediately「立即、馬上」。
> (A) 題目未詢問時間。
> (B) presentation「簡報」與題目中的 meeting「會議」看似有關，但並未詢問會議主題。
>
> 💡 應試者能理解問題內容，即使像問句使用較難句法─所有格代名詞，仍能選出適當的回應。

26. Can infer gist, purpose and basic context based on information that is explicitly stated in short spoken texts

Can understand a speaker's purpose or implied meaning in a phrase or sentence

Weren't the interns supposed to be working on this project?

(A) He's with another patient.
(B) I try to go walking every day.
(C) They still need additional training.

這些實習生不是應該要著手進行此專案嗎？

(A) 他正陪著另一位病人。
(B) 我試著每天去散步。
(C) 他們仍需要額外的訓練。

> **正解 (C)**
>
> 否定疑問句確認「這些實習生不是應該要著手進行此專案了嗎？」選項 (C) 回答他們仍需額外的訓練，they 代表題目中的實習生，藉此說明實習生沒做專案的原因。intern「實習生」，suppose to「應該」，work on「從事於、做某事」。
> (A) 不知道 he 是指誰。patient「病人、患者」。
> (B) walking 與題目中的 working 發音相似。go walking「散步」。
>
> 💡 應試者能推斷說話者的目的。
>
> 💡 即使說話者沒有直接回應或回應內容難以預測，應試者仍能理解說話者真正想表達的含意。

27. Can understand details in short spoken texts

What does the conference registration fee include?

(A) All sessions plus lunch.
(B) In Ballrooms 1 and 2.
(C) That's a reasonable rate.

這場會議的註冊費包含什麼？

(A) 所有的場次加上午餐。
(B) 在宴會廳 1 和 2。
(C) 這是合理的收費。

> **正解 (A)**
>
> 「What...?」詢問會議的註冊費包含什麼，選項 (A) 說明包含所有場次及午餐。conference「會議」，registration fee「註冊費」，include「包含」，session「場次」，plus「加上」。
> (B) ballroom「宴會廳」與 conference 看似有關，但題目並未詢問會議地點。
> (C) reasonable「合理的」，rate「費用」與題目中的 registration fee 看似有關，但題目並未詢問價格如何。
>
> 💡 應試者能理解問題詢問重點，並選出適當的回應。

28. Can understand a speaker's purpose or implied meaning in a phrase or sentence

You really should join that new fitness club.

(A) Basketball and tennis.
(B) Sorry I can't join you for dinner.
(C) Yes, I'd like to get more exercise.

你真該加入那間新開的健身俱樂部。

(A) 籃球和網球。
(B) 抱歉，我不能和你一起吃晚餐。
(C) 是的，我想多運動。

> **正解 (C)**
> 重點解說
> 題目提出「你真該加入那間新開的健身俱樂部。」選項 (C) 除了回答 yes，還表示「我想多運動」，表示回答者有加入健身俱樂部的意願。fitness「健康」。
> (A) basketball 和 tennis 與 fitness 相關，但題目並未詢問運動種類。
> (B) 題目與晚餐邀約無關。
>
> 💡 即使說話者沒有直接回應或回應內容難以預測，應試者仍能理解說話者真正想表達的含意。

29. Can understand a speaker's purpose or implied meaning in a phrase or sentence

Why do you want to sell your house?

(A) We provide home delivery.
(B) My new job's in London.
(C) A real estate agency.

為什麼你要賣掉你的房子？

(A) 我們提供宅配到府。
(B) 我的新工作在倫敦。
(C) 一位房屋仲介。

> **正解 (B)**
> 重點解說
> 「Why...?」詢問賣房子的原因，選項 (B) 說明因為新工作是在倫敦，暗指新工作的地點與目前住的地方不同，所以要賣房子。
> (A) home delivery「宅配」與題目的 house 有關，但答非所問。
> (C) real estate「房地產」，agency「仲介」與題目中的 sell your house 有關，但題目並未詢問是誰負責處理賣房子事宜。
>
> 💡 即使說話者沒有直接回應或回答內容難以預測，應試者仍能理解說話者真正想表達的含意。

30. Can understand a speaker's purpose or implied meaning in a phrase or sentence

Sir, please turn off your mobile phone for the rest of the flight.

(A) Flight eight sixty-seven to Tokyo.
(B) Oh, sorry, I didn't hear the announcement.
(C) Stay in the left lane.

先生，請在剩下的航程關閉你的手機。

(A) 飛往東京的 867 班機。
(B) 喔，抱歉，我沒有聽到公告訊息。
(C) 保持在左側車道。

> **正解 (B)**
> 重點解說
> 題目提到請對方「在剩下的航程關閉手機。」選項 (B) 先是致歉，並解釋沒有關機的原因為「沒聽到公告訊息。」turn off「關閉」，flight「航班」，announcement「公告」。
> (A) 題目與班機號碼及目的地無關。
> (C) 請注意，lane 的發音與 airplane 相近，可能會造成誤解。lane 在此是指車道，但此題與車道無關。
>
> 💡 即使說話者沒有直接回應或回答內容難以預測，應試者仍能理解說話者真正想表達的含意。

31. | Can understand a speaker's purpose or implied meaning in a phrase or sentence

Do we have to submit our budget report on Friday, or is Monday OK?

(A) It was pretty expensive.
(B) He was here a few days ago.
(C) Maria was firm about the deadline.

我們必須在週五繳交預算報告，還是週一也行？

(A) 這非常貴。
(B) 他幾天前在這裡。
(C) Maria 對截止時間很堅持。

重點解說

正解 **(C)**

題目詢問「我們必須在週五繳交預算報告，還是週一也行？」選項 (C) 說明「Maria 對於截止時間很堅持」，表示必須於週五繳交預算報告。have to「必須」，submit「繳交」，budget「預算」，firm「強硬的、堅持的」，deadline「截止時間」。

(A) expensive 與題目中的 budge 看似有關，但題目並未詢問某物是否昂貴。基本上預算不會用 expensive 形容，這個單字通常用於形容待售物品的價格。

(B) 選項與題目中的 Friday、Monday 有關，但題目並未詢問人物出現的時間點。

💡 即使說話者沒有直接回應或回應內容難以預測，應試者仍能理解說話者真正想表達的含意。

TEST 2

Questions 32 through 34 refer to the following conversation with three speakers.

M1: Hi, ❶ welcome to Springton Furniture. I'm Tom. How can I help you?

M2: Hi. I'd like to return a lamp I bought here a couple of weeks ago.

M1: OK. ❷ Do you have your receipt with you?

M2: Uh, no, actually. ❸ I must have lost it.

M1: Hmm. ❹ Usually we can only take returns with a receipt. Let me ask my manager. Excuse me, Sarah?

W : Yes, Tom?

M1: This gentleman wants to return a lamp, but doesn't have his receipt.

W : OK. Sir, ❺ I'm afraid all I can do is offer you in-store credit. You can use it at any of our locations.

請參考以下三人對話內容，回答第 32 至 34 題。

男1：你好，歡迎光臨 Springton 家具店。我是 Tom，有什麼我可以效勞的嗎？

男2：你好，我想將幾周前在這裡買的一盞檯燈退貨。

男1：好的，請問你有帶發票來嗎？

男2：呃…事實上，沒有。我一定是弄丟了。

男1：嗯…通常我們只能憑發票退貨，讓我與經理確認一下。不好意思，Sarah？

女 ：是的，Tom？

男1：這位先生想要將一盞檯燈退貨，但是他沒有發票。

女 ：了解。這位先生，我恐怕只能提供你店內抵用金，你可以在我們的任何店面使用它。

---

32.   Can understand details in extended spoken texts

Where are the speakers?

(A) At a supermarket
(B) At a furniture store
(C) At a clothing retailer
(D) At an automobile repair shop

說話者在哪裡？

(A) 超市
(B) 家具店
(C) 服飾零售店
(D) 汽車維修行

重點解說

正解 **(B)**

❶第一位男子說「歡迎光臨 Springton 家具行」迎接另一位男子，由此可知，對話是在家具行進行。furniture「家具」。

(C) retailer「零售商」。

(D) automobile「汽車」，repair「修理」。

💡 應試者能聽懂此段對話以理解對話發生的地點。

33. Can understand details in extended spoken texts

Why does Tom ask the woman for help?

(A) A receipt is missing.
(B) A computer is broken.
(C) A warranty is expired.
(D) An item is out of stock.

Tom 為何向女子請求協助？

(A) 發票不見了。
(B) 電腦壞了。
(C) 保固期過了。
(D) 有一樣商品缺貨了。

重點解說

正解 (A)
因男子想要退貨，Tom 詢問對方❷「你有帶發票來嗎？」對方回答❸「我一定是弄丟了。」Tom 接著說❹「通常我們只能憑發票退貨，讓我與經理確認一下。」由此可知，對方的發票不見了。receipt「發票」，must have ＋過去分詞常用來表示對過去某事的肯定，lost 在此為 lose「遺失、弄丟」的過去分詞。
(C) warranty「保固」，expire「到期、結束」。
(D) out of stock「缺貨」。

💡 應試者能理解對話中男子所提到的狀況細節。

34. Can understand details in extended spoken texts

What does the woman offer to do for the customer?

(A) Give him in-store credit
(B) Check a storage room
(C) Call another store
(D) Provide express delivery service

女子主動提供什麼給顧客？

(A) 提供他店內抵用金
(B) 檢查倉庫
(C) 打電話給另一家店
(D) 提供快遞服務

重點解說

正解 (A)
女子說❺「我恐怕只能提供你店內抵用金。」由此得知她只能提供店內抵用金給該名顧客，故選項 (A) 為正解。
(B) storage「儲藏」。
(D) express「快速的、特快的」，delivery「運送」。

💡 應試者能理解對話中女子所說的細節，藉此得知她採取什麼折衷方式。

Questions 35 through 37 refer to the following conversation.

請參考以下對話內容，回答第 35 至 37 題。

M: Hello, this is Don Simons. ❶ I have an appointment with Dr. Ramirez on Wednesday, but I'm afraid I have to reschedule.

男：妳好，我是 Don Simons。我與 Ramirez 醫生週三有約，但我恐怕必須要改時間了。

W: OK. When would you be able to come in?

女：好的，那你什麼時候可以過來？

M: How about on Thursday?

男：週四可以嗎？

W: ❷ Dr. Ramirez works at Brookside Medical Clinic on Thursdays. She's only in this office on Mondays and Wednesdays. You'll have to call them to schedule an appointment.

女：Ramirez 醫生每週四在 Brookside 醫療診所工作，她只有週一和週三會在這間診所。你必須要打電話給他們安排預約。

M: Oh, I see. ❸ Do you have their telephone number?

男：好的，我明白了。妳有他們的電話號碼嗎？

W: ❹ Yes, it's 555-0102. Be sure to let them know that you usually see Dr. Ramirez at this location.

女：有，電話號碼是 555-0102。請務必讓他們知道你通常在這邊由 Ramirez 醫生看診。

---

35. Can understand details in extended spoken texts

Why is the man calling?

男子打電話的目的是什麼？

(A) To inquire about a job
(B) To request a prescription
(C) To ask about business hours
(D) To reschedule an appointment

(A) 詢問工作
(B) 申請處方籤
(C) 詢問營業時間
(D) 重新安排預約時間

重點解說

正解 (D)

❶男子一開始便說明「我與 Ramirez 醫生週三有約，但我恐怕必須要改時間了。」由此可知，男子致電的原因是要將原訂週三的約診改時間。appointment「預約、約會」，reschedule「改時間、改行程」。
(A) inquire「詢問、打聽」。
(B) request「要求」，prescription「處方」。
(C) business hours「營業時間」。

💡 應試者能聽懂此段對話以理解男子致電的原因。

36. `Can infer gist, purpose and basic context based on information that is explicitly stated in extended spoken texts`

What does the woman say about Dr. Ramirez?

(A) She is presenting at a conference next week.
(B) She works at two different locations.
(C) She teaches at a medical school.
(D) She usually does not work on Wednesdays.

女子說了關於 Ramirez 醫生的什麼事情？

(A) 她下週將在會議上發表。
(B) 她在兩個不同的地點工作。
(C) 她在醫學院教課。
(D) 她週三通常不工作。

<table>
<tr><td rowspan="2">重點解說</td><td>

正解 (B)

❷女子提到「Ramirez 醫生每週四在 Brookside 醫療診所工作，她只有週一和週三會在這間診所。」由此可知，Ramirez 醫生在兩個不同的地方工作，故選項 (B) 為正解。medical「醫療的」，clinic「診所」，location「地點」。
(A) 對話中未提到 Ramirez 醫生下週要在會議上發表。present「表達、呈現」，conference「會議」。
(C) 對話未提到她在醫學院教課。
(D) 根據對話，Ramirez 醫生每週三是有工作的。

💡 應試者能理解對話中女子所提到的細節，進而推斷與 Ramirez 醫生相關的資訊。
</td></tr>
</table>

37. `Can understand details in extended spoken texts`

What does the woman give to the man?

(A) Directions to a medical center
(B) A Web site address
(C) A phone number
(D) A cost estimate

女子提供男子什麼？

(A) 前往醫療中心的路線
(B) 網站網址
(C) 電話號碼
(D) 成本估算

<table>
<tr><td rowspan="2">重點解說</td><td>

正解 (C)

❷女子說明 Ramirez 醫生每週四在另一個地點工作後，男子提問❸「妳有他們的電話號碼嗎？」女子回答❹「有，電話號碼是 555-0102。」由此可知，女子提供 Ramirez 醫生週四工作的診所電話號碼給男子，故選項 (C) 為正解。
(A) 對話中未提供到達某個地點的方向。direction「方向」。
(D) 對話中未提到成本估算。estimate「估算」。

💡 應試者能理解對話中女子所說的細節，藉此得知她提供男子什麼樣的資訊。
</td></tr>
</table>

TEST 2

Questions 38 through 40 refer to the following conversation.

M: Hi. ❶ Do you have a schedule of events here at the library?

W: Actually, ❷ we're holding an art show next weekend. We'll be showcasing paintings by local artists, and all of the pieces will be for sale. Here's a brochure with the information.

M: Thanks. Oh, ❸ and I see that the money raised will be used to start an after-school tutoring program in the area. That's great.

請參考以下對話內容，回答第 38 至 40 題。

男：妳好，請問妳有圖書館的各項活動時程表嗎？

女：其實，我們下週末將會舉辦一場藝術展。我們將會展示本地藝術家的畫作，而且所有的作品都會販售。這本手冊裡有活動訊息。

男：謝謝。對了，我注意到募款所得將會用來開辦當地一個課後輔導的計畫。真是太棒了。

38. Can infer gist, purpose and basic context based on information that is explicitly stated in extended spoken texts

Who most likely is the woman?

(A) A library employee
(B) A professor
(C) A café owner
(D) A museum curator

女子的身分最有可能是什麼？

(A) 圖書館職員
(B) 教授
(C) 咖啡廳老闆
(D) 博物館館長

重點解說

正解 (A)
男子詢問女子 ❶「請問妳有圖書館的各項活動時程表嗎？」由此可知，女子是在圖書館工作，故選項 (A) 為正解。
employee「員工」。
(D) curator「館長」。

💡 應試者能理解生活情境的相關單字，才能聽懂此段對話，並就內容推論女子從事何種行業。

39. `Can understand details in extended spoken texts`

What event will take place next weekend?

(A) A film screening
(B) An academic lecture
(C) A musical performance
(D) An art show

下週末將會舉行什麼活動？

(A) 電影放映
(B) 學術講座
(C) 音樂表演
(D) 藝術展

重點解說

正解 **(D)**

女子提到❷「我們下週末將會舉辦一場藝術展。」故選項 (D) 為正解。
(A) film「電影」，screening「放映」。
(B) academic「學術的」，lecture「講座、課」。
(C) musical「音樂的」，performance「表演」。

💡 應試者能理解對話中女子所提到的狀況細節。

40. `Can understand details in extended spoken texts`

What will the event's profits be used for?

(A) Purchasing new merchandise
(B) Offering an internship
(C) Creating a tutoring program
(D) Renovating part of a building

活動的收益將會用在什麼地方？

(A) 購買新的商品
(B) 提供實習
(C) 成立輔導計畫
(D) 翻新部份的建築物

重點解說

正解 **(C)**

男子提到❸「我注意到募款所得將會用來開辦當地一個課後輔導的計畫。」由此可知，選項 (C) 成立一個輔導計畫，為正確答案。raise「募集」，after-school「放學後」，tutor「輔導，指導」，profit「利潤、收益」。
(A) purchase「購買」，merchandise「商品、貨物」。
(B) internship「實習」。
(D) renovate「翻新、修復」。

💡 應試者能理解對話中男子所說的細節，藉此得知此活動收益將用於何處。

題目／中文翻譯

Questions 41 through 43 refer to the following conversation.

請參考以下對話內容，回答第 41 至 43 題。

M: Hi. Thank you for calling R&M Airport Shuttle Service. How can I help you?

W: Hello, my name is Sandra Johnson and ❶ I'm at the Crestville Regional Airport. I had a reservation to be picked up at one o'clock, but I don't see the shuttle here.

M: I'm so sorry, Ms. Johnson. I actually just spoke to the driver. ❷ There's some road construction near the airport, and she had to take a detour. The shuttle should be there in about five minutes.

W: Oh, great. I'll wait here then.

M: OK. ❸ To apologize for the inconvenience, we'll take 25 percent off your bill.

男：您好，感謝您致電 R&M 機場接駁服務。有什麼我可以幫您的嗎？

女：你好，我的名字是 Sandra Johnson，我在 Crestville 地區機場。我有預約一點的接送，但是我在這裡沒有看到接駁車。

男：真的很抱歉，Johnson 小姐。實際上我剛剛才和司機通話。機場附近有道路施工，所以她必須改道。接駁車應該再 5 分鐘左右就會到達。

女：喔，太好了。那我就在這裡等。

男：好的。很抱歉造成您的不便，我們將為您的帳單打 75 折。

41. Can understand details in extended spoken texts

Where is the woman?

(A) At a hotel
(B) At an airport
(C) At a car rental office
(D) At a train station

女子在哪裡？

(A) 旅館
(B) 機場
(C) 汽車租賃辦公室（租車公司）
(D) 火車站

重點解說

正解 (B)
女子自我介紹後便說明 ❶「我在 Crestville 地區機場」，由此可知說話者所在位置，故選項 (B) 為正解。regional「地區的」。
(C) rental「出租、租借的」。

💡 應試者能聽懂此段對話以理解女子所在的地點。

42. Can understand details in extended spoken texts

According to the man, what has caused a delay?

(A) **Road construction**
(B) Bad weather
(C) A scheduling mistake
(D) A mechanical problem

根據男子所言，什麼原因造成了延誤？

(A) **道路施工**
(B) 惡劣天氣（天候不佳）
(C) 調度有誤
(D) 機械問題

正解 (A)

男子說明❷「機場附近有道路施工，所以她必須改道。」此句的 she 指的是男子前一句提到的接駁車司機，故選項 (A) 為正解。construction「建設、工程」，detour「改道、繞路」。
(B) 對話中未提到天氣狀況。
(C) 對話中未提到調度有誤。
(D) mechanical「機械的」，對話中並未提到有機械相關問題。

💡 應試者能理解對話中男子所提及的細節。

43. Can understand details in extended spoken texts

What does the man say he will do?

(A) Contact his supervisor
(B) Issue a boarding pass
(C) **Apply a discount**
(D) Print a map

男子說他將會做什麼？

(A) 聯絡他的上司
(B) 發放登機證
(C) **使用折扣**
(D) 印出地圖

正解 (C)

男子說明❸「很抱歉造成您的不便，我們將為您的帳單打 75 折。」故選項 (C) 為最適切的答案。apologize「道歉、認錯」，inconvenience「不便、麻煩」，take...percent off「打…折」，apply「使用、運用」，discount「折扣」。
(A) contact「聯絡」，supervisor「上司」。
(B) issue「發行、頒發」，boarding pass「登機證」。

💡 應試者能理解對話中男子所說的細節，藉此得知他接下來將會做什麼。

Questions 44 through 46 refer to the following conversation.

M: Hi, Hannah. I have a meeting with the company president on Tuesday to discuss the budget. ❶ Since you're head of accounting, ❷ I was hoping you could present the earnings figures from last quarter.

W: Let me check... <u>I don't have anything scheduled that day.</u>

M: Great! Your input will really help us have a productive discussion. ❸ We're still working on the meeting agenda, and I'll send it to you as soon as it's finalized.

請參考以下對話內容，回答第 44 至 46 題。

男：妳好，Hannah。我週二要和公司總裁開會討論預算。因為妳是會計部的主管，我希望妳可以報告上一季的收益狀況。

女：讓我看一下⋯我那天沒有安排任何事。

男：太好了！妳的意見將會幫助我們進行一場有成效的討論。我們還在安排會議議程，一旦敲定我會立刻寄給妳。

---

44. Can understand details in extended spoken texts

Which department does the woman work in?

(A) Marketing
(B) Accounting
(C) Product development
(D) Human resources

女子在哪個部門工作？

(A) 行銷
(B) 會計
(C) 產品開發
(D) 人力資源

重點解說

正解 (B)

男子一開始先說明他要跟公司的總裁開會討論預算，接著說明❶「因為妳是會計部的主管」，由此可知，女子是在會計部門工作，故選項 (B) 為正解。president「總裁」。

💡 應試者能聽懂此段對話，才能得知女子在哪個部門工作。

45. Can infer gist, purpose and basic context based on information that is explicitly stated in extended spoken texts

Can understand a speaker's purpose or implied meaning in a phrase or sentence

What does the woman mean when she says, "I don't have anything scheduled that day"?

(A) She did not receive an invitation.
(B) She has finished interviewing candidates.
(C) She wants to revise a travel itinerary.
(D) She can give a presentation.

女子說「I don't have anything scheduled that day」代表什麼意思？

(A) 她沒有收到邀請。
(B) 她完成了求職者的面試。
(C) 她想修改旅遊行程。
(D) 她可以做報告。

重點解說

正解 (D)

❷男子提到希望女子能夠報告上一季的收益狀況，底線部分是女子的回覆「我那天沒有安排任何事。」由此可知，女子暗示她那天有空，能做報告，故選項 (D) 為正解。present「呈現」，earning「收入」，figure「數字」，quarter「季度」。

(A) receive「接收」，invitation「邀請」。
(B) candidate「候選人、應試者」。
(C) revise「修訂」，itinerary「行程」。

💡 應試者能理解對話中的上下文及大意。
💡 應試者能理解女子真正要表達的意思。

46. Can understand details in extended spoken texts

What will the man send to the woman?

(A) An agenda
(B) A manual
(C) A résumé
(D) A feedback form

男子將會寄什麼給女子？

(A) 議程
(B) 手冊
(C) 履歷表
(D) 回饋表單

重點解說

正解 (A)

男子向女子說明❸「我們還在安排會議議程，一旦敲定我會立刻寄給妳。」agenda「議程」，as soon as「立刻」，finalize「敲定、完成」。後半句的 it 指的是前半句中的 meeting agenda，故選項 (A) 為正解。

💡 應試者能理解對話中男子所說的細節，藉此得知他將會寄什麼給女子。

TEST 2

Questions 47 through 49 refer to the following conversation with three speakers.

M1 : Thanks for calling Komoto Advertising Agency. How can I help you?

M2 : Hi. ❶ This is Theodore Okuta, the real estate agent for the new office headquarters.

M1 : Oh, hello. Ms. Campbell was expecting your call. Let me transfer you to her now.

W : Hello. This is Ms. Campbell.

M2 : Hi, it's Theodore. ❷ I'm calling about the new office space. I wanted to let you know that I just e-mailed you the final version of the lease.

W : Great, thanks. I'll take a look at it shortly. Also, ❸ I'd like to discuss the timeline for the move. Ideally, we'd like to be in by the end of the year.

M2 : That shouldn't be a problem.

請參考以下三人對話內容，回答第 47 至 49 題。

男1：感謝您致電 Komoto 廣告經紀公司。有什麼我可以效勞嗎？

男2：你好，我是新辦公總部的房屋仲介 Theodore Okuta。

男1：喔，你好。Campbell 小姐正在等你的電話，讓我幫你轉接給她。

女 ：你好，我是 Campbell 小姐。

男2：妳好，我是 Theodore，我致電是為了新辦公室空間。我想讓妳知道，我已經把最終版本的租約用電子郵件寄給妳了。

女 ：太好了，謝謝，我稍後會看。另外，我想討論一下搬遷的時間表。理想的情況下，我們想要在年底前搬進去。

男2：這應該沒問題。

---

47. Can understand details in extended spoken texts

Who is Theodore?

(A) An architect
(B) A real estate agent
(C) A graphic designer
(D) A journalist

Theodore 是誰？

(A) 建築師
(B) 房屋仲介
(C) 平面設計師
(D) 記者

重點解說	正解 (B)
	❶男子自我介紹自己是新辦公總部的房屋仲介，故選項 (B) 為正解。real estate「房地產」，agent「代理人、經紀人」，headquarter「總部」。
	💡 應試者能聽懂此段對話以理解說話者的職業。

48. `Can understand details in extended spoken texts`

What does Theodore say he did?

(A) He scheduled a meeting.
(B) He took some photographs.
(C) He e-mailed a document.
(D) He visited a construction site.

Theodore 說他做了什麼？

(A) 他安排了會議。
(B) 他拍了一些照片。
(C) 他用電子郵件寄出文件。
(D) 他拜訪了施工地點。

重點解說

正解 **(C)**

❷男子先說明致電的目的是有關新的辦公室，並告知對方已寄出最終版本的租約，選項 (C) document「文件」代表租約，故為正解。version「版本」，lease「租約」。
(A) 對話中未提及要安排會議。
(B) photograph「照片」。
(D) construction site「施工地點」與新辦公室空間雖看似相關，但對話中並未提到要施工。

💡 應試者能理解對話中男子所提到的狀況細節。

49. `Can understand details in extended spoken texts`

What does the woman want to discuss?

(A) A staffing change
(B) A timeline
(C) A technical problem
(D) A budget

女子想要討論什麼？

(A) 人事變更
(B) 時間表
(C) 技術問題
(D) 預算

重點解說

正解 **(B)**

女子表示稍後會看一下男子寄來的租約，並提到 ❸「我想討論一下搬遷的時間表。」timeline「時間表」。
(A) staffing「人員配置」。
(C) technical「技術的」。

💡 應試者能理解對話中女子所說的細節，藉此得知她的討論主題。

Questions 50 through 52 refer to the following conversation.

M: Hello. I'm Ron Wells, the hiring manager here at Douglas Fashions. Thank you for coming in to interview for the sales associate position.

W: Of course. ❶ I'm excited about the possibility of working here. This is my favorite clothing shop.

M: Great. So, tell me about your previous sales experience.

W: Well, for the last six months I worked at a store in Fountain Mall. I really enjoyed it, ❷ but I quit because it took me over an hour to commute there.

M: I understand. Now, ❸ although you've already worked in sales, you'd still have to go through a monthlong training.

W: OK. No problem.

請參考以下對話內容，回答第 50 至 52 題。

男：妳好，我是 Douglas 時尚公司的招聘經理 Ron Wells，感謝妳前來參加銷售助理職務的面試。

女：當然。我很期待能有機會在這間公司工作，這是我最喜歡的服飾店。

男：很好，那麼請告訴我妳之前的銷售經驗。

女：嗯，過去六個月我在 Fountain 購物中心的一間店工作。我真的很喜歡，但是我辭職了，因為通勤要花超過一小時。

男：我明白了。雖然妳曾有過銷售經驗，但妳仍需要接受一個月的訓練。

女：好的，沒問題。

50. Can infer gist, purpose and basic context based on information that is explicitly stated in extended spoken texts

Where does the woman want to work?

(A) At a factory
(B) At a restaurant
(C) At a fitness center
(D) At a clothing store

女子想在哪工作？

(A) 工廠
(B) 餐廳
(C) 健身中心
(D) 服飾店

重點解說

正解 (D)
❶女子先說明自己很期待能有機會在這間公司工作，並接著說「這是我最喜歡的服飾店。」由此可知，女子想在服飾店工作。be excited about「某人對某事感到興奮」，possibility「可能性」。

💡 應試者能聽懂此段對話，並就內容推論女子應徵的公司。

51. Can understand details in extended spoken texts

Why did the woman leave her previous job?

(A) She began university studies.
(B) Her commute was too long.
(C) The company closed.
(D) The pay was low.

女子為什麼離開前一份工作？

(A) 她開始了大學課程。
(B) 她的通勤時間太長。
(C) 公司關閉了。
(D) 薪水低。

重點解說

正解 (B)

女子說明辭職原因❷因為通勤要花超過一小時。commute 在對話中為動詞「通勤」的意思，選項 (B) commute 作為名詞，也有同樣「通勤」的意思，故為正解。quit「辭職」。
(A) began 為 begin「開始」的過去式。
(C) 對話未提及公司經營狀況。
(D) 對話未提及薪水。

💡 應試者能理解對話中女子所提到的狀況細節。

52. Can understand details in extended spoken texts

What does the man explain to the woman?

(A) There are evening shifts.
(B) A uniform will be provided.
(C) Training will be necessary.
(D) The company is very small.

男子和女子解釋什麼？

(A) 有晚班。
(B) 會提供制服。
(C) 訓練是必須的。
(D) 公司規模很小。

重點解說

正解 (C)

男子說明❸「雖然妳曾有過銷售經驗，但妳仍需要接受一個月的訓練。」選項 (C) necessary「必要的」，表示受訓是必要的，故為正解。have to「必須」，monthlong「為期一個月」。
(A) 對話未提及是否有晚班，shift「班別」。
(B) uniform「制服」。
(D) 對話未提及公司的規模大小。

💡 應試者能理解對話中男子所說的細節，藉此得知他所說明的事項。

Questions 53 through 55 refer to the following conversation.

W: Hi, Ricardo. ❶ I'm calling because I'm working on the office supply order. ❷ Would you be able to look it over before I submit it?

M: Sure, but before I do, did you know that the supplier has sent out a new catalog? Some of the prices might have changed.

W: Oh, I didn't realize that. ❸ How can I get a copy of the new catalog?

M: ❹ I'll bring it over to you now.

W: OK, thank you. I'll check the prices right away. ❺ I'd like to submit this order before I leave for my business trip next week.

請參考以下對話內容，回答第 53 至 55 題。

女：你好，Ricardo。我打電話過來是因為我正在處理辦公室用品訂單，你可以在我遞交申請前看一下嗎？

男：當然可以，但是在我看之前，妳知道供應商寄送了新的目錄嗎？有些價格可能已經改變了。

女：喔，我並不知道。我要如何取得新版的目錄？

男：我現在拿來給妳。

女：好的，謝謝你。我會立刻確認價格。我想在下週出差前提交這份訂單。

---

53. Can understand details in extended spoken texts

What does the woman ask the man to do?

(A) Review an order
(B) Set up a computer
(C) Organize a conference
(D) Contact a client

女子請男子做什麼？

(A) 檢視訂單
(B) 安裝電腦
(C) 安排會議
(D) 聯絡客戶

正解 (A)

❶女子先說明致電的原因是關於辦公室用品的訂單，接著❷詢問男子是否能在她提交申請前，幫忙查看一下訂單內容。it 指的是❶提到的 office supply order。選項 (A) review 也有「檢查」之意，故為正解。office supply「辦公室用品」，look over「（快速）檢查、查看」，submit「提交」。
(B) set up「安裝、安排」。
(C) organize「組織、安排」。
(D) contact「聯絡」，client「客戶」。
💡 應試者能聽懂此段對話，以理解女子請男子做什麼。

54. Can understand details in extended spoken texts

What will the man bring to the woman?	男子將會帶什麼給女子？
(A) A catalog	**(A) 目錄**
(B) A calendar	(B) 月曆
(C) A list of suppliers	(C) 供應商名單
(D) A building directory	(D) 建築物指南

重點解說

正解 (A)

❸女子詢問要如何取得新版的目錄，男子說❹「我現在拿來給妳。」it 指的是❸女子詢問的目錄。catalog「目錄」，bring over「帶過來」。

(C) supplier「供應商」與對話中 supply「用品」讀音接近，要特別注意。

(D) directory「指南」。

💡 應試者能理解對話中男子所提到的狀況細節。

55. Can understand details in extended spoken texts

What does the woman plan to do next week?	女子下週打算做什麼？
(A) Send out a newsletter	(A) 寄出企業訊息
(B) Sign a contract	(B) 簽合約
(C) Go on a trip	**(C) 去旅行**
(D) Submit some slides	(D) 提交投影片

重點解說

正解 (C)

女子說明❺「我想在下週出差前提交這份訂單。」leave for「為…離開」，business trip「出差」。

(A) newsletter「機關、公司定期發行的消息資訊」。

(B) sign「簽署、簽名」，contract「合約」。

(D) slide「投影片」。

💡 應試者能理解對話中女子所說的細節，藉此得知她打算做什麼。

Questions 56 through 58 refer to the following conversation.

請參考以下對話內容，回答第 56 至 58 題。

W: Hi, Jeremy. ❶ My sales department wants to start an employee incentive program. I know that your department uses one, so I wanted your advice.

女：你好，Jeremy。我的業務部門想要啟動一個員工獎勵計畫，我知道你的部門有推行這樣的制度，所以我想詢問你的意見。

M: Sure. What would you like to know?

男：沒問題，妳想要知道什麼？

W: ❷ Employees will definitely be more eager to hit their sales goals if there's some sort of reward involved. But... ❸ what do you think the compensation should be?

女：公司若有提供某種獎勵，員工一定會更加熱切的達成他們的銷售目標。但…你認為獎勵應該是什麼呢？

M: Hmm...You spend more time with your team than I do.

男：嗯…妳和妳的團隊相處的時間比我多。

W: Right—I think they'd really enjoy earning additional vacation time.

女：也是，我認為他們會喜歡獲得額外的休假時間。

M: That's a great idea. ❹ Why don't you speak with Louis in Human Resources—he'd be able to give you more guidance about making extra vacation time an incentive.

男：這是個好主意。妳何不和人力資源部門的 Louis 討論？他可以給妳更多關於將額外假期當作獎勵的建議。

---

56. Can infer gist, purpose and basic context based on information that is explicitly stated in extended spoken texts

What are the speakers mainly discussing?

說話者主要在討論什麼事？

(A) A focus group
(B) Computer-use policies
(C) An upcoming merger
(D) Employee rewards

(A) 焦點團體
(B) 電腦使用政策
(C) 即將到來的合併
(D) 員工獎勵

> **重點解說**
>
> **正解 (D)**
> ❶女子說明她想在她的業務部門啟動獎勵計畫，因男子的部門有推行類似制度，所以想詢問男子的意見。男子詢問是想了解關於哪個部分，女子接著說明❷「公司若有提供某種獎勵，員工一定會更加熱切的達成他們的銷售目標。」由此可知，對話主要在討論員工獎勵。incentive「獎勵、激勵」，definitely「肯定」，eager「渴望的、熱切的」，hit「達成、達到」，sort「種類、類型」，reward「獎勵」，involve「包含、涉及」。
> (B) policy「政策」。
> (C) upcoming「即將到來的」，merger「合併」。
>
> 💡 應試者能聽懂此段對話，並就內容推論對話的大意。

57. Can understand a speaker's purpose or implied meaning in a phrase or sentence

What does the man imply when he says, "You spend more time with your team than I do"?

(A) The woman's team requires more staff.
(B) The woman should schedule fewer meetings.
(C) The woman is the best person to decide.
(D) The woman should have noticed a mistake.

男子說「You spend more time with your team than I do」，暗示了什麼？

(A) 女子的團隊需要更多職員。
(B) 女子應該減少安排會議。
(C) 女子是最佳的決策人選。
(D) 女子應該注意到了錯誤。

重點解說

正解 (C)

延續討論員工獎勵制度的話題，女子詢問男子❸獎勵應該是什麼，底線部分提到「妳跟妳的團隊相處的時間比我多。」由此可知，男子暗示女子應該會比他更清楚團隊的喜好，因此可推知男子認為應由女子自己決定要提供何種獎勵。選項 (C) the best person to decide 指的是最適合做決定的人選。
(A) 對話中未提到女子的團隊需要更多員工。require「需要」。
(B) 對話中未提到要減少會議安排。
(D) 對話中未提到有注意到任何錯誤。notice「注意」。

💡 應試者能理解對話中男子真正想要表達的意思。

58. Can understand details in extended spoken texts

What does the man advise the woman to do next?

(A) Speak with a colleague
(B) Research a competitor
(C) Download an application
(D) Attend a seminar

男子建議女子接下來要做什麼？

(A) 和一位同事交談
(B) 研究一個競爭者
(C) 下載一個應用程式
(D) 參加一個研討會

重點解說

正解 (A)

男子建議女子❹可與人力資源部門的人討論，以額外假期作為獎勵的相關注意事項。人資部屬於公司其中一個部門，故選項 (A) 為正解。colleague「同事」。
(B) research「做研究」，competitor「競爭者」。
(C) download「下載」；application「應用程式」，即 App。
(D) attend「參與、參加」，seminar「研討會」。

💡 應試者能理解對話中男子所說的細節，藉此得知他給予女子什麼建議。

Questions 59 through 61 refer to the following conversation.

W: Hi. Thanks for stopping by my booth at the technology expo today. ❶ As you can see, my company provides software that helps with accounting processes.

M: Wow. ❷ I just started my own business, and I've been looking for software to help with accounting.

W: Congratulations on your new business. Here's a brochure that has all the information you need about our product.

M: That's great. ❸ Is there a way I can test it out before purchasing it?

W: Of course. ❹ We offer a free 30-day trial, so you can see how it works and if it suits your needs.

請參考以下對話內容，回答第 59 至 61 題。

女：你好，感謝你今天在科技展覽會上光臨我的展位。如你所見，我的公司提供能協助會計流程的軟體。

男：哇，我最近才開始自己的事業，而且我一直在尋找有助於會計的軟體。

女：恭喜你成立新公司。這本手冊包含你所需關於我們產品的所有資訊。

男：太好了。是否可以讓我在購買前測試一下軟體嗎？

女：當然。我們提供 30 天免費試用，讓你可以了解它如何操作以及是否符合你的需求。

---

59. | Can understand details in extended spoken texts

What is being discussed?

(A) Appliances
(B) Some software
(C) Printers
(D) Television sets

本對話在討論什麼？

(A) 電器
(B) 軟體
(C) 印表機
(D) 電視機組

重點解說

正解 **(B)**

❶女子說明她的公司提供協助會計流程的軟體，由此可知，對話討論重點與軟體相關。software「軟體」，accounting「會計」，process「過程、程序」。

💡 應試者能聽懂此段對話，以理解對話所討論的主題為何。

60. `Can understand details in extended spoken texts`

What did the man recently do?

(A) He received a certificate.
(B) He published a book.
(C) He started a business.
(D) He renovated an office.

男子最近做了什麼？

(A) 他獲得了一張證書。
(B) 他出版了一本書。
(C) 他創立了事業。
(D) 他整修了一間辦公室。

> **重點解說**
>
> 正解 **(C)**
> ❷男子說明最近才開始自己的事業，故選項 (C) 為正解。
> (A) receive「接收、獲得」，certificate「證書」。
> (B) publish「出版」。
> (D) renovate「翻新、整修」。
>
> 💡 應試者能理解對話中男子所提到的狀況細節。

61. `Can understand details in extended spoken texts`

What does the woman say is available?

(A) Overnight shipping
(B) An extended warranty
(C) An online user manual
(D) A free trial

女子說可以提供什麼？

(A) 隔日送達
(B) 延長保固
(C) 線上用戶手冊
(D) 免費試用

> **重點解說**
>
> 正解 **(D)**
> 男子詢問女子❸是否可在購買前測試一下軟體，it 指的是女子在❶提到的 software。女子接續回答❹「我們提供 30 天免費試用，讓你可以了解它如何操作以及是否符合你的需求。」
> (A) overnight「一夜之間」，shipping「運送」。
> (B) extended「延長的」， warranty「保固」。
> (C) manual「手冊」。
>
> 💡 應試者能理解對話中女子所說的細節，藉此得知她公司能夠提供什麼服務。

Questions 62 through 64 refer to the following conversation and map.

W: ❶ I'm very excited to write about the annual restaurant festival—it's my favorite event in the city.

M: Me too. ❷ I'm glad our magazine editor sent us to cover this. ❸ According to the map on my phone, we should be there in a half hour.

W: That'll give me plenty of time to set up for my interviews with some of the local chefs.

M: Great. Oh—❹ on the map it looks like we'll be approaching a roundabout soon. We're on Cedar Lane right now, and you'll need to take Exit 3.

W: All right.

請參考以下對話及地圖，回答第 62 至 64 題。

女：我很開心能夠撰寫關於一年一度的餐廳節——這是我在這個城市中最喜歡的活動。

男：我也是。我很高興我們的雜誌編輯派我們來報導這個。根據我手機上的地圖，我們應該在半小內會抵達。

女：這讓我有足夠的時間來準備採訪一些當地的廚師。

男：太好了。喔…從地圖上看起來我們很快就會接近一個圓環。我們正位在 Cedar 巷，待會要走 3 號出口。

女：好的。

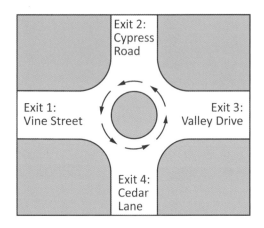

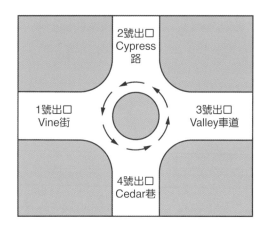

---

62. Can infer gist, purpose and basic context based on information that is explicitly stated in extended spoken texts

What event are the speakers going to attend?

(A) A concert
(B) A marathon
(C) An art show
(D) A restaurant festival

說話者要去參加什麼活動？

(A) 演唱會
(B) 馬拉松
(C) 藝術展
(D) 餐廳節

重點解說

正解 (D)

女子提到 ❶ 很開心能夠撰寫關於一年一度的餐廳節的文章，男子除了同意女子所說的之外，接續說明 ❸「根據我手機上的地圖，我們應該在半小時內會抵達。」由此可知，說話者將要參加餐廳節的活動，故選項 (D) 為正解。

💡 應試者能從對話提供的訊息中，推論說話者將要參與什麼活動。

63. | Can infer gist, purpose and basic context based on information that is explicitly stated in extended spoken texts |

Who most likely are the speakers? | 說話者最有可能是誰？

(A) Chefs | (A) 廚師
(B) Musicians | (B) 音樂家
(C) Investors | (C) 投資客
(D) Journalists | **(D) 新聞記者**

> 重點解說
>
> 正解 (D)
> 女子提到❶很開心能夠撰寫關於年度餐廳節的文章，接著男子提到❷「我很高興我們的雜誌編輯派我們來報導這個。」由此可推知，說話者在雜誌社工作，故選項 (D) journalist「新聞記者」為正解。editor「編輯」，cover「報導」。
>
> 💡 應試者能從對話提供的訊息中，推論說話者的職業。

64. | Can understand details in extended spoken texts |

Look at the graphic. Which road will the speakers take next? | 請看圖。說話者接下來要走哪一條路？

(A) Vine Street | (A) Vine 街
(B) Cypress Road | (B) Cypress 路
(C) Valley Drive | **(C) Valley 車道**
(D) Cedar Lane | (D) Cedar 巷

> 重點解說
>
> 正解 (C)
> 男子提到❹「從地圖上看起來我們很快就會接近一個圓環。我們正位在 Cedar 巷，待會要走 3 號出口。」看圖可得知，走 3 號出口會是接續走 Valley 車道。
>
> 💡 應試者能理解對話中男子所說的細節並對照圖表，藉此得知接下來將會走哪一條路。

Questions 65 through 67 refer to the following conversation and chart.

請參考以下對話及圖表，回答第 65 至 67 題。

W: Hi Chang-Ho, thanks for letting me visit your factory. ❶ When I saw your production numbers at the monthly corporate meeting for factory managers, I knew I had to come and see what I could learn from you. ❷ Any strategies for a fellow factory manager at Caldicott Industries?

女：你好 Chang-Ho，謝謝你讓我參觀你的工廠。當我在工廠經理的公司月會上看到你們的生產數據時，我知道我必須來看看我能從你這裡學習到什麼。有沒有可以給同為 Caldicott 企業工廠經理的策略方法呢？

M: You're welcome. Honestly, ❸ the secret to turning out so many toasters isn't only fancy equipment like people sometimes think—it's getting to know your workers.

男：不客氣。老實說，能生產這麼多烤麵包機的秘訣，不是只有靠人們以為的昂貴設備，而是要多認識妳的員工。

W: Oh, really?

女：喔，真的嗎？

M: Yes, it creates a positive and productive environment on the factory floor. Let's go out to the loading dock where you can meet some employees. ❹ Check the chart to make sure you have the right safety gear for the loading dock.

男：是的，這在廠房建立一個積極且高效的環境。讓我們去裝卸平台，在那裡妳可以見到一些員工。看一下這張圖表，確保妳有適合裝卸平台的安全裝備。

Safety Gear Requirements				
	Goggles	Ear protection	Hard hat	Foot protection
Factory floor		X		
Packaging room	X			
Loading dock				X
Supply room			X	

安全裝備要求				
	護目鏡	護耳罩	安全帽	足部防護
廠房		X		
包裝室	X			
裝卸平台				X
物料庫			X	

65. Can infer gist, purpose and basic context based on information that is explicitly stated in extended spoken texts

Why is the woman visiting the man's factory?

女子為什麼要參觀男子的工廠？

(A) To learn about management strategies
(B) To inspect some equipment
(C) To train new employees
(D) To enact a new guideline

(A) 學習管理策略
(B) 檢查設備
(C) 訓練新員工
(D) 實施新的規範

重點解說

正解 (A)

❶女子先說明參觀男子工廠的起因，接著詢問男子❷能提供任何策略方法給同樣身為工廠經理的她嗎？由此可知，女子想知道男子是如何經營管理工廠，提升生產量，故選項 (A) 為正解。production「生產」，corporate「公司的」，strategy「策略」，fellow「同事的」，industry「產業」。

(B) inspect「檢查」，equipment「設備」。
(C) train「訓練」。
(D) enact「實行、實施」，guideline「方針」。

💡 應試者能從對話提供的訊息中，推論女子參觀工廠的原因。

66. | Can understand details in extended spoken texts

What reason does the man give for his results?

(A) Hiring outside consultants
(B) Building relationships with staff
(C) Investing in the most recent technology
(D) Maintaining diverse suppliers

針對他的成效，男子提出什麼理由？

(A) 聘用外部顧問
(B) 和員工建立關係
(C) 投資最新的科技
(D) 維持多元化的供應商

重點解說

正解 (B)

❸男子說明「能生產這麼多烤麵包機的秘訣，不是只有靠人們以為的昂貴設備，而是要多認識妳的員工。」選項 (B) build relationships「建立情誼」意思接近 get to know「了解」，staff「員工」意思近於 workers，故為正解。secret「秘密、秘訣」，turn out「製造」，fancy「昂貴的」。
(A) consultant「顧問」。
(C) invest「投資」，recent「最新的」。
(D) maintain「維持」，diverse「多樣的」。

💡 應試者能理解對話中男子所提到的狀況細節。

67. | Can understand details in extended spoken texts

Look at the graphic. What safety gear does the woman need to wear?

(A) Goggles
(B) Ear protection
(C) A hard hat
(D) Foot protection

請看圖表。女子要穿戴哪一個安全裝備？

(A) 護目鏡
(B) 護耳罩
(C) 安全帽
(D) 足部防護

重點解說

正解 (D)

❹男子說「看一下這張圖表，確保妳有適合裝卸平台的安全裝備。」對照表格，在裝卸平台所需的裝備為選項 (D) 足部防護。

💡 應試者能理解對話並對照圖表，藉此得知女子需要什麼裝備。

Questions 68 through 70 refer to the following conversation and building layout.

W: Good afternoon, ❶ I'm from Star Locksmiths. I'm here about a door that isn't locking properly.

M: Thank you for coming so quickly. It's a major security concern that one of our doors doesn't lock.

W: Yes, I understand. I know which door it is, so I'll just head over there.

M: Thanks. And it'd be great if this could be fixed before noon. ❷ Employees who work in the other buildings will need to use that door to enter the cafeteria.

W: OK, I'll get started right away.

M: Thank you. ❸ Just remember to keep your visitor's badge visible at all times.

請參考以下對話及建築物平面設計圖,回答第 68 至 70 題。

女:午安,我來自 Star 鎖行。我來這裡是因為有扇門無法正常上鎖。

男:很高興妳這麼快就過來。其中一扇門無法上鎖是重大的安全問題。

女:是的,我明白。我知道是哪一扇門,那麼我就直接過去。

男:謝謝,如果可以在中午前修好那就太好了。在另一棟樓工作的員工需要從那扇門進入餐廳。

女:好的,我馬上開始。

男:謝謝。請記得一直將妳的訪客證配戴於明顯處。

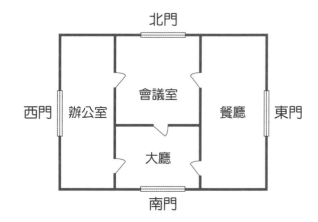

68. **Can infer gist, purpose and basic context based on information that is explicitly stated in extended spoken texts**

What most likely is the woman's job title?

(A) Custodian
(B) Locksmith
(C) Landscaper
(D) Parking attendant

女子的職稱最有可能是什麼?

(A) 管理員
(B) 鎖匠
(C) 景觀設計師
(D) 泊車員

重點解說

正解 (B)

❶女子一開始便介紹公司名稱,並接著說明來此的原因是因為有扇門無法上鎖,因此可推論女子的職稱為選項 (B) locksmith「鎖匠」。

💡 應試者能從對話提供的訊息中,推論女子的職稱。

69. Can infer gist, purpose and basic context based on information that is explicitly stated in extended spoken texts

Look at the graphic. Which door are the speakers discussing?

(A) The North Door
(B) The East Door
(C) The South Door
(D) The West Door

請看圖。說話者在討論哪一扇門？

(A) 北門
(B) 東門
(C) 南門
(D) 西門

重點解說

正解 (B)
男子提到希望能在中午前修好門鎖，因為 ❷「在另一棟樓工作的員工會需要從那扇門進入餐廳。」對照平面圖，唯一一扇能從外面直接進入餐廳的門只有 East Door。cafeteria「餐廳」。

💡 應試者能理解對話中男子所提到的狀況細節，並推論討論的事項。

70. Can understand details in extended spoken texts

What does the man remind the woman to do?

(A) Display her badge
(B) Store her belongings
(C) Submit her time sheet
(D) Validate her parking pass

男子提醒女子做什麼？

(A) 展示識別證
(B) 存放財物
(C) 提交時間表
(D) 查驗停車證

重點解說

正解 (A)
男子提到 ❸「記得一直將妳的訪客證配戴於明顯處。」選項 (A) 用 display「展現、顯現」表示要將證件展示出來讓其他人看見，故為正解。visitor's badge「訪客證」，visible「可見的、顯眼的」。
(B) store 在此為動詞「存放、收納」，belongings「財物」。
(C) time sheet「時間表」。
(D) validate「查驗、核可」，parking pass「停車證」。

💡 應試者能理解對話中男子所說的細節，藉此得知他提醒女子注意什麼。

Questions 71 through 73 refer to the following news report.

And now for local news. ❶ Renovations began today on the Northridge Town Hall. ❷ All new additions to the Town Hall were designed by Byron Lang. Mr. Lang is famous for using dramatic columns and arches in his architectural work, features that he will also incorporate into this building. Officials are expecting the building to reopen next year. ❸ Once that happens, tours will be given every weekend, so that town residents can come and see the changes.

請參考以下新聞報導,回答第 71 至 73 題。

現在是本地新聞。Northridge 市政廳今天起開始整修。市政廳所有新增建的部分都是由 Byron Lang 所設計。Lang 先生以在建築作品中採用宏偉的柱子和拱門聞名,並將會把這樣的特徵融入這座建築裡。官員們期待這座建築明年可以重新開放。一旦開放了,每個週末將會提供參觀行程,讓城鎮的居民可以過來看看這些改變。

71. Can infer gist, purpose and basic context based on information that is explicitly stated in extended spoken texts

What is the news report mainly about?

(A) A museum exhibit
(B) A holiday parade
(C) A building renovation
(D) A sports competition

這則新聞報導的主旨是什麼?

(A) 博物館展覽
(B) 假日遊行
(C) 建築物整修
(D) 運動競賽

重點解說

正解 (C)
說話者說 ❶「Northridge 市政廳今天起開始整修。」由此可知本篇新聞主要在說明建築物整修的消息,故選項 (C) 為正解。renovation「整修」。
(A) exhibit「展覽、展示」。
(B) parade「遊行」。
(D) competition「競爭」。

💡 應試者能理解產業領域的相關單字,以聽懂此段新聞並推論本篇主旨。

72. Can infer gist, purpose and basic context based on information that is explicitly stated in extended spoken texts

Who is Byron Lang?

(A) A travel agent
(B) An architect
(C) A city official
(D) An athlete

Byron Lang 是誰？

(A) 旅行社人員
(B) 建築師
(C) 市府官員
(D) 運動員

> **重點解說**
>
> 正解 (B)
>
> ❷ 提到市政廳所有新增建的部分都是由 Byron Lang 設計，他以在建築作品中採用宏偉的柱子和拱門聞名，故選項 (B) architect「建築師」為正解。addition「擴建部分」，be famous for「以…著名」，dramatic「戲劇性的、引人注目的」，column「柱子」，arch「拱門」，architectural「建築的」。
>
> 💡 應試者能理解產業領域的相關單字，以聽懂此段新聞並推論人物的職業。

73. Can understand details in extended spoken texts

What does the speaker say will be provided next year?

(A) Extra parking
(B) Weekend tours
(C) Souvenirs
(D) Job opportunities

說話者說明年會提供什麼東西？

(A) 額外的停車位
(B) 週末導覽
(C) 紀念品
(D) 工作機會

> **重點解說**
>
> 正解 (B)
>
> 新聞報導中提到市政廳預計明年會重新開放，接著 ❸ 說「一旦開放了，每個週末將會提供參觀行程。」once「一旦」，that 指的是市政廳重新開放。
>
> 新聞報導中並未提到 (A) 額外的停車空位、(C) 紀念品及 (D) 工作機會。
>
> 💡 應試者能理解說話者所說的細節，藉此得知明年會提供什麼。

TEST 2

Questions 74 through 76 refer to the following announcement.

Members of the press, ❶ I'm delighted to announce that Zepler Automobiles will be releasing the Y100 electric car on the market soon. ❷ The Y100 will be unlike any other electric car because the battery can be fully charged in only three hours. ❸ This is the shortest charging time of any electric car out there. The Y100 won't be available for a few more months, but ❹ we're opening a waiting list for interested customers. They can add their names to the online waiting list and one of our representatives will be in touch.

請參考以下發表內容,回答第 74 至 76 題。

媒體同業們,我很高興宣布 Zepler 汽車即將於市場上推出 Y100 電動汽車。Y100 將不同於其他電動車,因為只要三個小時電池就可以完全充飽,這是市面上所有電動汽車中充電時間最短的。還要再幾個月 Y100 才會上市,但我們將開放預約登記給有興趣的顧客,他們可以在線上登記表填入姓名,我們將會有專人聯繫。

74. | Can understand details in extended spoken texts

What product is the speaker discussing?　　　　　　　說話者正在討論什麼產品?

(A) An electric car　　　　　　　　　　　　　　**(A) 電動車**
(B) A mobile phone　　　　　　　　　　　　　　(B) 手機
(C) A washing machine　　　　　　　　　　　　(C) 洗衣機
(D) A refrigerator　　　　　　　　　　　　　　(D) 冰箱

重點解說

正解 (A)

說話者說 ❶「我很高興宣布 Zepler 汽車即將於市場上推出 Y100 電動汽車。」由此可知本篇發表會討論的產品為電動汽車,故選項 (A) 為正解。automobile「汽車」,release「推出」,electric「電動的」。

💡 應試者能理解說話者所說的細節,藉此得知討論的主題。

75. Can understand details in extended spoken texts

Why does the speaker say a product is unique?

(A) It is the smallest model available.
(B) It is the least expensive model available.
(C) Its motor is very quiet.
(D) Its battery charges quickly.

說話者為什麼說產品是獨特的？

(A) 這是可用的最小型號。
(B) 這是可用的最便宜型號。
(C) 它的馬達非常安靜。
(D) 它的電池充電很快。

正解 **(D)**

❷提到「Y100 將不同於其他電動汽車，因為只要三個小時電池就可以完全充飽。」接著❸補充說明指出此款電動汽車充電時間最短，故選項 (D) 為正解。unlike 與 unique「獨特」相關，battery「電池」，charge「充電」。
(A) model「型號」。
(B) least「最少、最小」。
(C) motor「引擎、馬達」。

💡 應試者能理解說話者所提到的細節，藉此得知此款商品獨特之處。

76. Can understand details in extended spoken texts

What does the speaker say the listeners can do?

(A) Put their names on a waiting list
(B) Submit their reviews online
(C) Participate in a product demonstration
(D) Assemble an item independently

說話者對聽者說他們可以做什麼？

(A) 把名字填入登記名單中
(B) 線上提交評論
(C) 參加產品展示
(D) 獨立組裝物品

正解 **(A)**

❹提到「我們將開放預約登記給有興趣的顧客，他們可以在線上登記表填入姓名，我們將會有專人聯繫。」其中第二句的 they 指的是第一句提到的 interested customers，故選項 (A) 為正解。waiting list「候補名單、登記名單」，representative「代表、代理人」，be in touch「聯繫」。
(C) participate「參與」，demonstration「示範、操演」。
(D) assemble「組裝、組合」，independently「獨立地」。

💡 應試者能理解說話者所說的細節，藉此得知聽者可以做些什麼。

重點解說

重點解說

TEST 2

題目／中文翻譯

Questions 77 through 79 refer to the following telephone message.

Hi, Percy. ❶ I'm calling to check in about the glassmaking workshop that Grace Tao and I are running next Monday at the community center. Most of the planning's already done—❷ we've decided on the glass project our students will work on, and I've sent you an outline for the workshop. ❸ There is one issue though—twenty students is a lot… there are only two of us. It'd be difficult for us to conduct a hands-on workshop with that many people, but we're also available on Tuesday. Can you call me back to discuss this further?

請參考以下電話留言，回答第 77 至 79 題。

你好，Percy。我打來是要確認我和 Grace Tao 下週一要在社區中心開辦的玻璃製作工作坊。大部分的計畫都已經完成了，我們已經決定了學生們要製作的玻璃項目，我剛剛也寄了工作坊的綱要給你。但是有一個問題，20 名學生太多了…我們只有兩個人。我們很難和這麼多人一起進行手作工作坊，但我們週二也有空檔。可以請你回電給我進一步討論這件事情嗎？

77. Can understand details in extended spoken texts

What is the speaker planning for next week?

(A) An awards ceremony
(B) A poetry reading
(C) A gardening lecture
(D) A glassmaking workshop

說話者計畫下週做什麼？

(A) 頒獎典禮
(B) 詩歌朗讀會
(C) 園藝講座
(D) 玻璃製作工作坊

重點解說

正解 (D)

說話者說❶「我打來是要確認我和 Grace Tao 下週一要在社區中心開辦的玻璃製作工作坊。」由此可知說話者正在為下週的工作坊做規畫，故選項 (D) 為正解。check in「確認」，glassmaking「玻璃製作」，workshop「工作坊」，community center「社區中心」。

💡 應試者能理解說話者所說的細節，藉此得知她下週的計畫。

78. `Can understand details in extended spoken texts`

What does the speaker say she sent to the listener? | 說話者說她寄給聽者什麼？

(A) An outline
(B) A credit card number
(C) A pamphlet
(D) A coupon

(A) 綱要
(B) 信用卡號碼
(C) 小冊子
(D) 優惠券

重點解說

正解 (A)

❷ 提到「我們已經決定了學生們要製作的玻璃項目，我剛剛也寄了工作坊的綱要給你。」由此可知說話者寄給聽者工作坊的綱要，故選項 (A) 為正解。outline「綱要、大綱」。

💡 應試者能理解說話者所說的細節，藉此得知她寄給聽者什麼。

79. `Can infer gist, purpose and basic context based on information that is explicitly stated in extended spoken texts`

`Can understand a speaker's purpose or implied meaning in a phrase or sentence`

Why does the speaker say, "but we're also available on Tuesday"?

(A) To ask for a budget increase
(B) To confirm attendance
(C) To complain about a scheduling conflict
(D) To suggest holding an additional class

說話者為什麼說「but we're also available on Tuesday」？

(A) 要求提高預算
(B) 確認出席
(C) 抱怨行程安排混亂
(D) 建議再加開一堂課

重點解說

正解 (D)

❸ 女子提到有個狀況想要討論，因為有 20 個人參與，但只有兩位講師。對講師而言，很難在這麼多學生的情況下進行手作課程。說話者底線部分提到「但我們週二也有空檔。」由此可推知，說話者建議新增一班，將學生分成兩班上課，故選項 (D) 為正解。issue「問題」，conduct「進行」，hands-on「親手做的」，hold「舉行」，additional「額外的」。

(A) ask for「要求」。
(B) confirm「確認」，attendance「出席」。
(C) complain「抱怨」，conflict「衝突」。

💡 應試者能根據上下文去推論說話者所說的大意及目的。

💡 應試者能理解說話者真正想表達的意思。

Questions 80 through 82 refer to the following instructions.

❶ This online tutorial is created by PRG Electronics Company to help you understand how to discard the hard drive from your old computer. The first step is to remove the hard drive from inside your laptop computer. Next, ❷ print a shipping label from our Web site. Then, affix the label you printed on a padded envelope and place the hard drive in it. Finally, take the package to your local post office. ❸ For every hard drive returned, we offer a ten percent discount on your next purchase from us.

請參考以下指示，回答第 80 至 82 題。

此線上教學是由 PRG 電子公司製作，旨在幫助你了解如何丟棄舊電腦的硬碟。第一個步驟是從筆記型電腦裡面移除硬碟，接下來從我們的網站列印託運單標籤。然後，將您印出的標籤貼在氣泡信封袋上，並且把硬碟放入其中。最後，將包裹帶到你在地的郵局。針對每個寄回的硬碟，我們提供下次購物九折的優惠。

80. Can understand details in extended spoken texts

What type of business created the tutorial?

(A) A post office
(B) A community college
(C) An electronics company
(D) A paper goods manufacturer

什麼類型的企業製作了教學？

(A) 郵局
(B) 社區大學
(C) 電子公司
(D) 紙用品製造商

重點解說

正解 (C)

說話者說 ❶「此線上教學是由 PRG 電子公司製作，旨在幫助你了解如何丟棄舊電腦的硬碟。」由此可知這是由電子公司所製作，故選項 (C) 為正解。tutorial「教學」，electronics「電子」，discard「丟棄」。
(D) manufacturer「製造商」。

💡 應試者能理解說話者所說的內容，藉此得知是什麼類型的產業製作了教學。

81. Can understand details in extended spoken texts

According to the speaker, what should the listeners print out?

(A) A shipping label
(B) A manual
(C) An invoice
(D) Installation directions

根據說話者，聽者應該要列印什麼？

(A) 託運單標籤
(B) 手冊
(C) 發票
(D) 安裝指示

重點解說

正解 **(A)**

❷提到「從我們的網站列印託運單標籤。」由此可知聽者應該要列印託運單標籤。shipping label「託運單標籤」。
(D) installation「安裝」，direction「指導」。

💡 應試者能理解說話者所說的內容，藉此得知聽者需要做什麼。

82. Can understand details in extended spoken texts

What does the speaker offer to the listeners?

(A) A warranty
(B) A discount
(C) Free accessories
(D) Express delivery

說話者提供聽者什麼？

(A) 保固
(B) 折扣
(C) 免費配件
(D) 快遞

重點解說

正解 **(B)**

❸提到「針對每個寄回的硬碟，我們提供下次購物九折的優惠。」return「返回、歸還」，discount「折扣」，purchase「購買」。
(C) accessory「配件、配飾」。
(D) express「快速的」。

💡 應試者能理解說話者所說的細節，藉此得知聽者會得到什麼。

PART 4

Questions 83 through 85 refer to the following excerpt from a meeting.

Hello, everyone. ❶ I'm Sophia Buckner, head of security services at the company. I'm here to remind you of a company security policy and to inform you of a change. OK, first, ❷ I want to remind everyone that it's against company policy to remove work documents from the building unless you get special permission from your supervisor. Second, ❸ we're making a change regarding access to the building. ❹ From now on, doors will be locked at all times, not just after hours, so you'll always need to use your key cards to enter.

請參考以下會議摘錄，回答第 83 至 85 題。

大家好，我是公司的安全部主管 Sophia Buckner。我在這裡要提醒各位公司的安全政策並且通知你們有所變動。好的，首先我要提醒各位，除非有經過上司的許可，否則從辦公大樓拿走工作文件是違反公司政策。其次，我們將針對大樓通行管制做一些改變。從現在起，所有的門不只有下班後才上鎖，而會一直保持上鎖狀態，所以你們會需要使用你們的門禁卡才能進入大樓。

83. | Can understand details in extended spoken texts

What department does the speaker work in?　　　說話者在哪一個部門工作？

(A) Accounting　　　　　　　　　　　　　(A) 會計
(B) Legal　　　　　　　　　　　　　　　　(B) 法務
(C) Security　　　　　　　　　　　　　**(C) 安全**
(D) Human Resources　　　　　　　　　　(D) 人力資源

> **重點解說**
>
> 正解 (C)
> 說話者自我介紹❶「我是公司的安全部主管 Sophia Buckner。」由此可知說話者在安全部門工作。
> (B) 在公司企業中，legal 有「法務部」的意思。
>
> 💡 應試者能理解說話者所說的內容，藉此得知她在哪個部門工作。

84. Can understand details in extended spoken texts

What does the speaker say the listeners need permission to do?

(A) Meet in a designated area
(B) Remove work documents
(C) Bring guests into the building
(D) Sign client contracts

說話者說聽者需要得到許可才能做什麼？

(A) 在指定區域見面
(B) 帶走工作文件
(C) 帶訪客進入大樓
(D) 簽署客戶合約

正解 **(B)**

❷提到「我要提醒各位，除非有經過上司的許可，否則從辦公大樓拿走工作文件是違反公司政策。」由此可知要將公司文件從辦公室帶走需要主管同意。remind「提醒」，against「違反、與…相反」，unless「除非」，permission「允許」，supervisor「上司、管理者」。
(A) designated「指定的」。

💡 應試者能理解說話者所提到的狀況細節。

85. Can understand details in extended spoken texts

What change does the speaker mention?

(A) Doors will now be locked.
(B) Management groups will be reorganized.
(C) A cafeteria will offer breakfast.
(D) A computer system will be upgraded.

說話者提到什麼改變？

(A) 現在門將會上鎖。
(B) 管理小組將會重組。
(C) 餐廳將會提供早餐。
(D) 電腦系統將會升級。

正解 **(A)**

女子先提到❸「我們將針對大樓通行管制做一些改變。」接著說明❹「從現在起，所有的門不只有下班後才上鎖，而會一直保持上鎖狀態。」由此可知，大樓的門現在隨時都是上鎖的。regarding「關於」，access「通道、途徑」，at all times「隨時」，after hours「下班後」。
(B) reorganize「重新組織」。

💡 應試者能理解說話者所說的細節，藉此得知公司安全政策有什麼樣的改變。

Questions 86 through 88 refer to the following telephone message.

Hi, Noemie, I'm calling about some customer service issues. ❶ Paper production has been steadily increasing over the past year. ❷ According to the most recent survey results, our customers do like the quality of our 100 percent recycled paper. However, ❸ I've been receiving complaints from clients about late deliveries because YS Delivery Service cannot fulfill our orders on time. ❹ It may cost us more, but we should definitely resolve this issue. <u>You're familiar with Fox International Deliveries, aren't you?</u> I've heard good things about them.

請參考以下電話留言，回答第 86 至 88 題。

你好，Noemie，我打電話來是要詢問一些客戶服務的問題。在過去的一年中，紙類的生產量穩定成長。根據最新的調查結果顯示，我們的客戶很喜歡我們百分之百回收再生紙張的品質。然而，我一直收到客戶對於延遲交貨的投訴，原因在於 YS 貨運公司無法準時完成我們的訂單。這或許會讓我們的成本增加，但是我們絕對該解決這個問題。你很熟悉 FOX 國際運送，不是嗎？我聽說他們還不錯。

86. Can infer gist, purpose and basic context based on information that is explicitly stated in extended spoken texts

What type of business does the speaker work in?　　說話者在什麼類型的企業工作？

(A) Automobile sales　　　　　　　　　　　(A) 汽車銷售
(B) Interior design　　　　　　　　　　　　(B) 室內設計
(C) Food distribution　　　　　　　　　　　(C) 食品配送
(D) Paper manufacturing　　　　　　　　**(D) 紙類製造業**

重點解說

正解 (D)

說話者說❶「在過去的一年中，紙類的生產量穩定成長。」此外，他接著在❷提到我們百分之百回收再生紙張，由此可知說話者的公司在生產紙類，故選項 (D) 為正解。production「生產量」，steadily「穩定地」。
(B) interior「內部」。
(C) distribution「分配」。

💡 應試者能理解產業領域的相關單字，以聽懂此段對話並推論說話者的公司產業類別。

87. `Can understand details in extended spoken texts`

According to the survey results, what do customers like about the speaker's company?

(A) **The quality of its products**
(B) The location of its branches
(C) Its dedication to customer satisfaction
(D) Its innovative advertisements

根據調查結果，客戶喜歡說話者公司的什麼？

(A) **產品品質**
(B) 分部地點
(C) 致力於客戶滿意度
(D) 它的創新廣告

重點解說

正解 (A)

❷提到「根據最新的調查結果顯示，我們的客戶很喜歡我們百分之百回收再生紙張的品質。」由此可知顧客喜歡這家公司產品的品質，故選項 (A) 為正解。according to「根據」，quality「品質」，recycle「回收」。
(B) branch「分部、分行」。
(C) dedication「致力」，satisfaction「滿意」。
(D) innovative「創新的」，advertisement「廣告」。

💡 應試者能理解說話者所提到的狀況細節。

88. `Can infer gist, purpose and basic context based on information that is explicitly stated in extended spoken texts`
`Can understand a speaker's purpose or implied meaning in a phrase or sentence`

What does the speaker imply when he says, "You're familiar with Fox International Deliveries, aren't you"?

(A) **He wants to change service providers.**
(B) He wants the listener to give a presentation.
(C) He wants to promote the listener to a new role.
(D) He wants to merge with another company.

說話者說「You're familiar with Fox International Deliveries, aren't you?」，暗示了什麼？

(A) **他想要更換服務供應商。**
(B) 他想讓聽者做簡報。
(C) 他要提拔聽者一個新職務。
(D) 他要和另一間公司合併。

重點解說

正解 (A)

說話者先提到❸「客戶對於延遲交貨的投訴，原因在於 YS 貨運公司無法準時完成我們的訂單。」說明了現在狀況，並提議❹絕對要解決這個問題，接著詢問聽者底線部分，暗指說話者有意要更換送貨廠商，故選項 (A) 為正解。fulfill「完成」，definitely「絕對」，resolve「解決」。
(C) promote「提拔」。
(D) merge「合併」。

💡 應試者能就說話者所說的細節及上下文內容做推論。
💡 應試者能理解說話者真正所要表達的意思。

題目/中文翻譯

Questions 89 through 91 refer to the following advertisement.

Are you planning to visit family or friends this upcoming holiday season? The new transport company, Roadbus, is offering incredible prices on trips between Penstown and many major cities! ❶ Our buses all have free Wi-Fi, so you can stay connected on your trip back home. ❷ Travel can be stressful, and train tickets are expensive. Roadbus is here to help. ❸ Visit our Web site at www.Roadbus.com to get ten percent off your online booking!

請參考以下廣告，回答第 89 至 91 題。

你打算在即將到來的假期探望家人或朋友嗎？新的運輸公司 Roadbus 為往來 Penstown 和其他主要城市的旅行提供令人難以置信的價格！我們的巴士都有免費 Wi-Fi，所以你在回家的旅途中也能隨時上網。旅行可能會讓人有壓力，且火車票很昂貴，Roadbus 在此幫助你。前往我們的官網 www.Roadbus.com 可享線上訂票九折的優惠！

89. Can understand details in extended spoken texts

What can the listeners receive at no cost?

(A) Parking
(B) Beverages
(C) Internet access
(D) Extra space

聽者可以免費獲得什麼？

(A) 停車
(B) 飲料
(C) 連線上網
(D) 額外空間

重點解說

正解 (C)

題目中的 no cost 指的是不需任何花費，說話者提到 ❶「我們的巴士都有免費 Wi-Fi，所以你在回家的旅途中也能隨時上網。」由此可知，聽者可以免費使用網路，故選項 (C) 為正解。Wi-Fi「無線網路」，access「（使用某物的）權利」。

💡 應試者能理解說話者所提到的狀況細節。

90.

Can infer gist, purpose and basic context based on information that is explicitly stated in extended spoken texts

Can understand a speaker's purpose or implied meaning in a phrase or sentence

What does the speaker imply when he says, "train tickets are expensive"?

(A) **The listeners should not take the train.**
(B) The listeners should not attend an event.
(C) The listeners should obtain approval for an expense.
(D) The listeners should travel in another season.

說話者說「train tickets are expensive」，暗示了什麼？

(A) **聽者不應該搭火車。**
(B) 聽者不應該出席活動。
(C) 聽者應該取得費用的許可。
(D) 聽者應該在其他的季節旅行。

重點解說

正解 (A)

說話者先提到❷「旅行可能會讓人有壓力」，底線部分接著說火車票很貴。在此，說話者暗指火車昂貴的票價會讓原本旅行的壓力又更加重，由此推知他認為聽者不應該搭火車。stressful「有壓力」。
(B) attend「出席」。
(C) obtain「取得」，approval「許可、同意」，expense「費用」。

💡 應試者能就說話者所說的細節及上下文內容做推論。

💡 應試者能理解說話者真正所要表達的意思。

91.

Can understand details in extended spoken texts

Why are the listeners encouraged to visit a Web site?

(A) To apply for funding
(B) **To receive a reduced price**
(C) To fill out a survey
(D) To submit a form

為什麼要鼓勵聽者前往官網？

(A) 申請資金
(B) **獲得折扣價**
(C) 填寫問卷
(D) 提交表格

重點解說

正解 (B)

❸說明上 Roadbus 官網，可享線上訂票九折的優惠，故選項 (B) reduced price「折扣價」為最適切的答案。
(A) apply for「申請」，funding「資金」。
(C) fill out「填寫」。
(D) submit「遞交」。

💡 應試者能理解說話者所提到的狀況細節。

TEST 2

Questions 92 through 94 refer to the following excerpt from a meeting.

Good afternoon. ❶ Your CEO here at Yorktown Department Store requested that my marketing firm make some recommendations based on current fashion trends. This will help you make smart decisions about what clothes to sell and when. ❷ We get information about the latest fashion trends by following screen and music stars on social media, just as your customers do. ❸ We noticed that you've been selling your line of winter clothes too early in the year. Most celebrities don't start wearing winter outfits until mid-October, but you've been displaying your winter collections beginning in September. ❹ I'd recommend holding the winter line until October.

請參考以下會議摘錄,回答第 92 至 94 題。

午安。你們 Yorktown 百貨公司的執行長,要求我的行銷公司針對現今潮流趨勢提供一些建議。這將會幫助你們就銷售什麼衣服以及何時銷售做出明智的決定。就像你們的客戶一樣,我們藉由追蹤社群媒體上的影視及音樂明星來得知最新時尚趨勢消息。我們注意到你們每年都太早販售冬季系列的服飾。大多數名人直到 10 月中旬才開始穿冬裝,但你們從 9 月就開始展示冬裝系列。我會建議將冬季系列延至 10 月。

92. | Can infer gist, purpose and basic context based on information that is explicitly stated in extended spoken texts

What industry does the speaker work in? | 說話者在什麼產業工作?

(A) Electronics | (A) 電子業
(B) Finance | (B) 金融業
(C) Marketing | **(C) 行銷**
(D) Tourism | (D) 旅遊業

重點解說

正解 (C)

說話者說❶「你們 Yorktown 百貨公司的執行長,要求我的行銷公司針對現今潮流趨勢提供一些建議。」由此可知,說話者是在行銷產業工作。

💡 應試者能理解產業領域的相關單字以聽懂此段會議摘錄,並推論聽者是在什麼產業。

93. Can understand details in extended spoken texts

How does the speaker say she stays informed about current trends?

(A) **She follows social networking sites.**
(B) She analyzes consumer reviews.
(C) She reads industry journals.
(D) She interviews movie stars.

說話者說她如何掌握現今趨勢？

(A) **她追蹤社群網站。**
(B) 她分析消費者評論。
(C) 她閱讀產業期刊。
(D) 她採訪電影明星。

重點解說

正解 (A)

題目中的 stay informed 指的是「保持消息靈通」，說話者提到❷「藉由追蹤社群媒體上的影視及音樂明星來得知最新時尚趨勢消息」，選項 (A) 為最適切的答案。social networking sites「社群網站」。

(B) analyze「分析」，consumer「消費者」。

(C) journal「雜誌、期刊」。

💡 應試者能理解說話者所提到的狀況細節。

94. Can understand details in extended spoken texts

What does the speaker suggest changing?

(A) Where to open a new office
(B) **When to sell certain products**
(C) How to arrange a display
(D) What brands to carry

說話者建議改變什麼？

(A) 開設新辦公室的地點
(B) **銷售特定產品的時間點**
(C) 如何陳列商品
(D) 銷售哪個品牌

重點解說

正解 (B)

❸提到「我們注意到你們每年都太早販售冬季系列的服飾。」接著❹說明「我會建議將冬季系列延至 10 月。」由此可知，說話者建議對方改變銷售特定商品的時間。notice「注意」，recommend「建議」，hold「延遲」。

(C) arrange「安排」，display「展示」。

(D) brand「品牌」，carry「發展、攜帶」，在此表「銷售、代理」該品牌。

💡 應試者能理解說話者所說的細節，藉此得知她建議改變什麼。

Questions 95 through 97 refer to the following telephone message and menu.

Hi, this is Josh Romoff. ❶ I'm calling to confirm my catering order for my son's graduation party. ❷ I ordered the meat platter... uh, that's a large meat platter, because we'll have a lot of people there. Also, ❸ I requested that two people from your catering company serve the food to the guests on the day of the party. ❹ I'm wondering what time I should expect them to come. Please call me back at this number when you get this message. Thanks.

請參考以下電話留言與菜單，回答第 95 至 97 題。

你好，我是 Josh Romoff。我打電話來是要確認我兒子畢業派對的外燴訂單。因為我們將會有很多人在場，所以我訂了肉類拼盤…嗯，一個大份的肉類拼盤。另外，我有要求你們的外燴公司安排兩個人在派對當天服務現場賓客。我想知道他們幾點會到呢？請在收到這則訊息後回撥這個號碼給我。謝謝。

SANCHEZ' CATERING COMPANY
MENU

	MEDIUM	LARGE
MEAT PLATTER	$300	$500
VEGETABLE PLATTER	$250	$400

SANCHEZ' 外燴公司
菜單

	中份	大份
肉類拼盤	$300	$500
蔬菜拼盤	$250	$400

95. Can understand details in extended spoken texts

What event is the speaker planning?

(A) A board meeting
(B) A retirement party
(C) A graduation party
(D) A job fair

說話者正在計畫什麼活動？

(A) 董事會議
(B) 退休派對
(C) 畢業派對
(D) 就業博覽會

正解 (C)

說話者說❶「我打電話來是要確認我兒子畢業派對的外燴訂單。」由此可知說話者要舉辦一場畢業派對。
(A) board「董事會、委員會」。
(B) retirement「退休」。
(D) fair「園遊會、博覽會」。

💡 應試者能理解說話者所提到的狀況。

96. Can understand details in extended spoken texts

Look at the graphic. How much will the speaker pay for his food order?

(A) $250
(B) $300
(C) $400
(D) $500

請看圖。說話者要為他的食物訂單付多少錢？

(A) 250 元
(B) 300 元
(C) 400 元
(D) 500 元

重點解說

正解 (D)

❷ 提到「因為我們將會有很多人在場，所以我訂了一個大份的肉類拼盤。」對照菜單，大份的肉類拼盤價格為 500 元，故選項 (D) 為正解。

💡 應試者能理解電話留言中男子所提到的狀況細節，並將電話留言及菜單中的資訊連結。

97. Can understand details in extended spoken texts

What does the speaker ask about?

(A) Whether he is eligible for a discount
(B) When food servers will arrive
(C) Which serving utensils are included
(D) Whether food containers must be returned

說話者詢問什麼？

(A) 他是否有資格獲得折扣
(B) 上菜服務人員何時會抵達
(C) 哪些分菜餐具會包含在內
(D) 食物容器是否須歸還

重點解說

正解 (B)

❸ 先說明已有要求外燴公司安排兩個人，在派對當天服務現場賓客，接著問❹他們幾點會到。句中的 them 指的是前面提及外燴公司的兩名員工。由此可知，說話者想詢問外燴公司的員工何時會抵達他家。request「要求」，wonder「想知道」，server「服務人員」。

(A) whether「是否」，eligible「有資格的」。
(C) serving utensil「分菜餐具」，include「包括」。
(D) container「容器」。

💡 應試者能理解說話者所說的細節內容。

題目/中文翻譯

Questions 98 through 100 refer to the following announcement and advertisement.

Hi, everyone. ❶ I just met with our financial advisers. ❷ There were some unanticipated problems with the electrical work, and I had to pay the contractor for additional hours in order to meet our August twelfth opening date. This means we can no longer afford to offer as many special events this summer. Since the park will likely be busier on weekends, ❸ I've decided to cancel the recurring Wednesday event. We still need to let our advertising firm know so they can update our promotional materials. ❹ I plan to give them a call this afternoon.

請參考以下公告與廣告，回答第 98 至 100 題。

大家好，我剛與我們的財務顧問會面。因為電力工程出現一些無預期的問題，我必須付錢給承包商加班，以趕上我們 8 月 12 日的開幕日。這意味著今年夏天我們再也負擔不起舉行這麼多的特別活動。由於樂園在週末時可能會比較忙碌，我決定取消每週三的例行活動。我們仍需要讓我們的廣告公司知道，以便他們可以更新我們的宣傳素材。我打算今天下午打電話給他們。

LEBBINSVILLE AMUSEMENT PARK
Grand Opening: August 12

Special Events All Summer!

Wednesdays	Comedy Special
Thursdays	Magic Show
Fridays	Music Performance
Saturdays	Parade

LEBBINSVILLE遊樂園
盛大開幕：8 月 12 日

整個夏天的特別活動！

週三	喜劇特演
週四	魔術秀
週五	音樂表演
週六	遊行

98. Can infer gist, purpose and basic context based on information that is explicitly stated in extended spoken texts

Who most likely is the speaker?

(A) A park owner
(B) A journalist
(C) An electrician
(D) A graphic designer

說話者最有可能是誰？

(A) 樂園老闆
(B) 記者
(C) 電工技師
(D) 平面設計師

正解 (A)

重點解說

說話者說❶「我剛與我們的財務顧問會面。」接著說明❷「因為電力工程出現一些無預期的問題，我必須付錢給承包商加班，以趕上我們 8 月 12 日的開幕日。」由說話者的內容，加上遊樂園開幕廣告，可得知她是遊樂園的老闆。financial adviser「財務顧問」，unanticipated「意料之外的」，electrical「電力的」，contractor「承包商」，additional「額外的」。

(C) 雖然 electrical work 與 electrician「電工」有關，但根據上下文，說話者要與財務開會，還要付款給承包商，可合理推斷說話者為老闆。

💡 應試者能就上下文去推斷說話者的身分。

99. Can understand details in extended spoken texts

Look at the graphic. Which special event was canceled?　　請看圖表。哪一項活動被取消？

(A) The Comedy Special　　　　　　　　　　　　**(A) 喜劇特演**
(B) The Magic Show　　　　　　　　　　　　　　(B) 魔術秀
(C) The Music Performance　　　　　　　　　　　(C) 音樂表演
(D) The Parade　　　　　　　　　　　　　　　　(D) 遊行

重點解說

正解 (A)

說話者提到❸「我決定取消每週三的活動。」根據廣告，每週三的活動為 Comedy Special。recurring「重複發生的」。

💡 應試者能理解公告中男子所提到的狀況細節，並對照圖表以得知哪個活動項目被取消。

100. Can understand details in extended spoken texts

What will the speaker do this afternoon?　　　　　說話者今天下午將要做什麼？

(A) Introduce a guest　　　　　　　　　　　　　(A) 介紹一位來賓
(B) Show a video　　　　　　　　　　　　　　　(B) 展示影片
(C) Describe a contest　　　　　　　　　　　　　(C) 描述一場比賽
(D) Make a phone call　　　　　　　　　　　**(D) 打電話**

重點解說

正解 (D)

說話者提到❹「我打算今天下午打電話給他們。」這邊的他們指的是前面提及的 advertising firm「廣告公司」。
(A) introduce「介紹」。
(C) describe「描述」，contest「比賽」。

💡 應試者能理解說話者所說的細節內容，藉此得知她將做什麼。

TEST 2

TOEIC® Listening and Reading Test
Official Test-Preparation Guide Vol. 8 Listening Part
TOEIC®聽力與閱讀測驗官方全真試題指南 Vol. 8 聽力篇

發 行 人　　邵作俊
作 　 者　　*ETS*®
編 　 譯　　*TOEIC*® 臺灣區總代理 忠欣股份有限公司
出 版 者　　*TOEIC*® 臺灣區總代理 忠欣股份有限公司
地 　 址　　台北市復興南路二段 45 號 2 樓
電 　 話　　(02) 2701-7333
網 　 址　　www.toeic.com.tw

出版日期／中華民國 112 年 5 月
再版日期／中華民國 113 年 3 月
定 　 價／新台幣 650 元
本書如有缺頁、破損或裝訂錯誤，請寄回更換。

聽力測驗全真試題 (1) 練習用答案卡

1 聲明與簽名：請閱讀下方聲明文字，並全部抄寫於下方橫線中。

答案卡上記載的資料皆為我本人所親筆填寫。我同意遵守 TOEIC 測驗規定及違規處理規定，也不會以任何形式向他人洩漏或公開 TOEIC 測驗部分或全部的題目。

簽名 Signature :

測驗日期 Date :　　　／　　　／

◎重要注意事項 IMPORTANT NOTICE
● 請勿劃記試題本 Marking on the test book is prohibited.
● 請勿跨區作答 Please work on the assigned section only.

2 准考證號碼 ADMISSION NUMBER

3 國家代碼 COUNTRY CODE

4 語言代碼 LANGUAGE CODE

5 職稱 OCCUPATION

學校／公司名稱 SCHOOL / COMPANY NAME

所在城市 CITY

6 測驗地點 TESTING LOCATION

試場 TESTING ROOM

7 試題本號碼 TEST FORM

試題本流水編號 TEST BOOK SERIAL NUMBER

聽力測驗 LISTENING (Parts 1 - 4)

1–100

閱讀測驗 READING (Parts 5 - 7)

101–200

聽力測驗全真試題 (2) 練習用答案卡

1 聲明與簽名：請閱讀下方聲明文字，並全部抄寫於下方橫線中。

聲明與簽名：請閱讀下方聲明文字，並全部抄寫於下方橫線中。
答案卡上記載的資料皆為我本人所親筆填寫。我同意遵守 TOEIC 測驗規定及達規處理規定，也不會以任何形式向他人洩漏或公開 TOEIC 測驗部分或全部的題目。

◎ 重要注意事項 IMPORTANT NOTICE
● 請勿劃記試題本 Marking on the test book is prohibited.
● 請勿跨區作答 Please work on the assigned section only.

簽名 Signature：

測驗日期 Date：　　　／　　　／

2 准考證號碼 ADMISSION NUMBER

3 國家代碼 COUNTRY CODE

4 語言代碼 LANGUAGE CODE

5 職稱 OCCUPATION

學校 / 公司名稱 SCHOOL / COMPANY NAME

所在城市 CITY

6 測驗地點 TESTING LOCATION

試場 TESTING ROOM

7 試題本號碼 TEST FORM

試題本流水編碼 TEST BOOK SERIAL NUMBER

聽力測驗 LISTENING (Parts 1 - 4)

閱讀測驗 READING (Parts 5 - 7)

MP3

**Audio tracks
for download**

收錄兩套完整聽力測驗全真試題，
音檔音軌獨立，可用電腦、手機播放

請輸入網址
https://publishing.chunshin.com.tw/download/TOEIC_LR_OG8
**或用手機掃描QR Code，輸入下載碼後，
即可下載MP3音檔聆聽。**

下載碼：　　　**ffadea6fca**

桌上型或筆記型電腦下載

1. 請在瀏覽器輸入上述網址，進入本書音檔下載網頁。

2. 在右方的空白方框內輸入「下載碼」後，點擊「登入下載」。

3. 閱讀「音檔下載使用同意書」並點選「同意」後，點擊右方「下載」按鈕，開始下載。

4. 下載檔案解壓縮後，即可在解壓縮後的資料夾中看到聽力測驗題目MP3音檔，請對照書中目錄或題號旁的耳機圖示，依圖示的數字找到對應的題目。

手機或平板電腦下載

1. 掃描QR Code或於瀏覽器輸入上述網址，進入本書音檔下載網頁。

2. 輸入「下載碼」並點擊「登入下載」。

3. 閱讀「音檔下載使用同意書」並點選「同意」按鈕。

4. 下載
   - **iOS裝置**：請點擊「下載」，待下載完成後，至資料夾中的「下載項目」，點擊所下載的zip檔解壓縮。
   - **Android裝置**：請點擊「下載」，選擇儲存路徑並下載後，至「下載管理員」或儲存路徑，點擊所下載的zip檔解壓縮。

5. 在解壓縮後的資料夾中看到聽力測驗題目MP3音檔，請對照書中目錄或題號旁的耳機圖示，依圖示的數字找到對應的題目。

※注意事項

1. 不支援Windows XP、Windows 7、Windows 8、Internet Explorer（IE）所有版本。

2. 每組「下載碼」可跨裝置、跨平台使用，共能下載5次。

3. 下載檔案前，請確認您的電腦或手機儲存空間足夠；並於網路訊號良好、網路速度穩定、無流量限制等情況下再開始下載音檔。

4. 音檔下載有任何疑問，請來信客服信箱：service@examservice.com.tw